Step into a Whole World of Weird...

STRANGE
Tales *are* These

seven short stories

by
Sheila LaNewton

 Book Publishing.com

Design, typesetting and publishing by UK Book Publishing

www.ukbookpublishing.com

ISBN: 978-1-917329-98-9

STRANGE
Tales *are* These

seven short stories

For my Mum

EDITH ENTWISTLE

… who always wanted her name in LIGHTS

~

For my Son

PHIL NEWTON

…whose motto was

Never Let the Bastards Grind you Down

~

Miss you both - always

Contents

Introduction 1

Foreword 3

1. It's Raining Cats and Dogs 5

2. Que Sera, Sera – Riding the Wave of Change 21

3. A Snake in the Grass 39

4. My Father's Tweed Suit 55

5. Mighty Red 73

6. À La Carte Alley 93

7. The Dissociative Associate 107

Afterword & Acknowledgements 133

About the Author 138

Introduction

An introduction to Sheila's short story collection, "Strange Tales are These".

A. Winter is the leader/facilitator of one of two 'local-to-the-northeast' creative writing groups that the author is an active member of.

A. Winter has been – still is – and will always be – a boon to the author's writing and creativity. There is so much to thank her for.

~

Welcome to the debut collection of Sheila LaNewton! A dazzling array of short stories told by energised, witty and eccentric narrators. Enter seven lively and sometimes surreal worlds where gritty dialect mixes with vivid poetic descriptions - you will be intrigued and astounded and never bored: There is the journey of a fame-hungry protagonist longing for cleanliness; a veterinarian whose life is changed by a strange storm; black magic imprisons a daughter in her father's body and tweed suit. A chef discovers that kindness pays whilst a teacher's misjudged comments lead to terrible consequences. These are contemporary tales with some unexpected visitors - beware of lingering too long in a pay toilet! A fascination with the friendships between creatures and their humans will leave you wanting more from this exciting, original writer.

A. Winter

Foreword

It's always lovely when a former student comes to publish their work and this is no exception. I had the privilege of tutoring Sheila, and I was always impressed with her willingness to learn, take on feedback, and to ask questions of her own work which pushed her writing further and further. The stories she shared during the course had a careful balance of whimsy, insight, and drama, which is often hard to achieve, all packaged with a natural instinct for the craft of writing. I'm sure these 'strange tales' will delight readers in the same way and will leave them wanting more of Sheila LaNewton.

Dr Mike Hollows BA (Hons), MA, PGCert, AFHEA, PhD

Lecturer in Further and Higher Education

Tutor – Professional Writing Academy and New Writing North

Author - (pen name) M J Hollows

IT'S RAINING CATS AND DOGS

It's Raining
Cats and Dogs

'Yes, viewers, I kid you not,' the blonde weather presenter on the BBC News said, arms akimbo, fingers fluttering, 'It's happening, all over the world. So many weather fronts. It'll take more than umbrellas, wellies and cagoules to stop you from getting wet and windswept today. *And* it's the same story for the next few days, according to the forecast. We have hurricanes in Honolulu and Hong Kong, Storm Zoey in Zanzibar. There are terrible tornadoes in Tel Aviv and Toronto and snowstorms in Siberia. Those strong winds are widespread, globally – and curiously, they're all lifting skyward, in heavy, thundery gales. We may even be treated to a tornado in one little area in the northeast of the UK. Keep an eagle eye on Pleasantree Woods near the North Sea coast. I guarantee it'll be a sight for sore eyes.' She pointed at the weather map, finger-circling that little knobbly bit on the border between North Tyneside and Northumberland.

* * *

I already knew about the disturbance in the weather around the area where I live, having treated myself to a land-and-sky telescope a month or so ago. The stars are my passion, though I have some interest in nature-watching around and about the countryside. I'm a stalker of wildlife, if you really must know. I do draw a line at peeking through bedroom windows with my viewfinder!

I live so very near to Pleasantree Woods, in Northumberland, I can almost touch it, with or without a telescope.

I'd been stargazing way above the North Sea - when down and to the right, I noticed a swirling, whirling wind blowing the choppy waves of the water. An extraordinary sight that became more unreal as I adjusted the lens of the telescope. The whiteness of the wind turned a grisly grey, spreading, rotating. I spied the T-shape of a horizontal vortex. I could sense the wind upsurging, banging against my unopened window. Lightning struck, flashing and flaring. Could I see signs of the Northern Lights glowing in pinks, greens and aquamarines?

Yes, I thought, *I can. All the colours of the rainbow. Vivid, rich and stunning.*

The screams of the warning siren competed with the roar of an intense, fierce tornado, shaped like a huge upside-down magic mushroom. Hail thundered down in icy globes as big as footballs. Dust and flying debris raced over the sea toward land. Cold. Wet. Harsh.

I watched in awe, my ears buzzing with deafening crackles and bangs; my eyes scrunched and wrinkled in the fierce light. It was like the biggest firework display ever. But terrifying.

After about half an hour, the mushroom tipped upright, slowly billowing outward and upward. I hoped upon hope it really was a tornado – and not an atomic bomb.

It hit the ground running. Earth flew up into a mound of crackling, lightning-ravaged volcanic activity. Steaming and flaring, like it was glaring right at me. Thunder roared like Thor wielding his hammer. Before my very eyes, a colossal mound of fiery-red flames lit up the landscape in front of the woodland, growing larger and wider. Shrubs and grassy sods flew up, pulled clear by the thick, ethereal trunk of the whipping, rolling tornado. A mountainous mound of rock appeared in its wake.

The ground trembled and shook. Earthquake-like tremors forced the earth to grumble, the trees to sway, the leaves to fall. It began to rain. It was as though the heavens had released their doors to open the show. And what a show it was. What a performance.

It was raining cats and dogs. Literally! Myriad glorious beasts tumbled down to their new terrain in the drenching downpour. Plummeted earthward in foggy billows and hazy waves. Dense crowds of felines and canines thumped to the ground in Pleasantrees Woods. Tiny pups and kittens; dogs, bitches, toms and queens – some small, many medium, lots large. Wagging, happy dog tails; crazy static-electric cat tails. Mewls and howls abounded, competing with deafening thunderclaps, sheets of sleet and heavy hailstones. Strangely, there were no fatalities or injuries. Not one.

All pet-lovers know, cats are well renowned for landing with four paws on the ground, safe and sound. Dogs, on the other hand can be clumsy. Most of them, though, adopted a "drop, parachute-in, roll" style, tongues hanging out, wet and drooling, barking loudly in delight.

Have you ever heard anybody say, 'Never seen anything like it in my life'? It often seems a bit of a stretch, somehow, yeah? Well, on this occasion, it was true. I mean, nothing could ever top the splendour of a sight so special. Not a thing.

I saw it all for real from my telescope viewfinder. The world saw it "live" on television.

I was in awe. Whole nations must have been flabbergasted.

***

The news presenter smiled at the camera, saying, 'This astounding woodland critter colony is to be renamed, "Mutt-n-Mog Mound" according to local sources. You can see why. Dogs and cats are raining in, (pardon the pun) in their thousands.'

The news and weather presenters waxed lyrical - on and on - about this amazing phenomenon. They said it would be grand for tourism in the northeast. That people would travel from around the country - and indeed the world. They'd pack their picnics, sit on rugs and blankets. People would come from far-and-wide to see them, taken in by the cute kittens and pawing pups. They'd buy water, pop and wine – all to take in the sights and sounds of these furry friends from foreign parts and nearby nooks and crannies.

* * *

Once the heavens closed, the sky reducing its watery overload to spits and spots, the canines and felines set off merrily. At a running jump, they ran through the trees, down the slope, toward the river. As they disappeared out of sight, burger and hot dog trucks pulled up at the nearside of Mutt-n-Mog Mound, alongside ice-cream vans. I was surprised not to see a funfair appearing out of the blue.

The roaring trade matched the fast-flowing torrent of the river. It was no more than a babbling brook before the storm. Now, as the sun went down in the turbulent sky, the river became busy, like it was in some sort of mad rush. The humans seemed more interested in the goodies they could buy and munch on. It was as though the cats and dogs had lost their novelty. How fickle people can be.

I realised the tornado was moving away from the woods. Slowly but surely. Weaving a lazy hip-sway back out to sea. The wind dropped to a steady breeze.

I set my telescope sights over the trees to the sand and stones of the shore. Was I the only person in the world watching these critters lick and slurp at the water? It seemed so, until I heard the buzzing of helicopters, the rattling of drones, arriving to spy on the thrills and spills. Unheeded, I did my own snooping with my own trusty telescopic machine.

Left to their own devices, the felines and canines sat on the flinty edges of the water, raising their voices like they were chanting songs of praise to their gods. Maybe they were.

The cats lay on small rocks along the edges, pawing at pebbles and tasting the holy water. They lifted their heads to the dwindling sun, crying, 'MEOW'. The dogs splashed and swam. In and out of the river, they leaped, howling like wolves, barking "BOW-WOW" like … well …dogs! They too, reared their heads upward to the heavens, singing their hymns.

As I looked down on the wonderful scene - the setting sun a fiery red ball, the trees swaying in the shadows – I noticed an ominous oak, glaring at me with menacing intent, from a wizened visage as old as the hills. Its face was set in the centre of the oak's trunk. It changed its expression into a warm smile as I gazed upon it. *Ah. I've made a friend,* I thought. Then I realised the tree hadn't been annoyed with me; he'd been angry with the drones and the helicopter. That thought radiated out and into the sky. There were more drones now. More helicopters too.

My stately old oak tree curled his top lip. My animals snarled and yelped. Yes, I said "my" because, already, I felt a connection with these creatures and this foliage. It was uncanny. They certainly disliked the intrusion from the flying machines that hovered and zipped their way over the hurtling waters. The old oak waved his branches furiously. The wind sighed in exasperation. The pups and dogs yipped and yapped in displeasure. The kits and cats hissed in annoyance.

I began to wonder if this awe-inspiring oak might be the original Tree of Life, the World Tree of the Anglo-Saxons.

Why? It was as though he was a controlling force of nature. Maybe he was a friend of the Earth Mothers – the Sisters of Wyrd. I mean, why not? There was a magical quality to the air. I could feel it. My dogs and cats could feel it, I was sure.

Next thing I saw, all the other trees in the wood bowed low as the felines and canines crept toward the great oak, lowering their heads in a submissive gesture. *Wow! Mother Nature herself might be at work here in Mutt-n-Mog Mound.* I got to wondering whether that new trendy nickname would ever stick. I mean, Pleasantree Woods is grand enough for me. No gimmicks needed.

Prayers over, the mutts and mogs made their way back to the cooling volcanic mound, playing and larking around. Dachshunds and Pomeranians fooled around with Siamese and Rag Dolls. German Shepherds and Cocker Spaniels acted out with Maine Coons and Abyssinians. Dazzled by the red circle of the sun setting, I watched as cats congregated together on top of the Mound. I gathered it must be the turn of the felines to keep watch while the canines slept. Perhaps it would be vice versa during daylight.

As dusk approached with rapid loss of sunlight, I couldn't *not* watch. In fact, I spied on the vigilant puss-cats all night long; listened to the snuffles and snores of dogs curled up under trees and bushes. And I thought I couldn't bear to be just an onlooker. Who knew how long these animals would hang around? Being a veterinary, I could be of use. By the end of the night, I'd vowed to offer my services here at Pleasantree Woods, in my free time.

And I did, the very next day.

I've always believed in the power of three. Three is the magic number. My 'three' are, my veterinary skills, my love of animals and my adoration of nature. Whatever I put into the world, I could take out three-fold. *Yes please*, I thought.

* * *

Life got interesting at the woods and the riverside very quickly. The café was renovated to make it into a Visitor Centre. Guided tours were conducted hourly between nine and six, every day. The BBC were right to think that 'Mutt-n-Mog Mound' would attract people to the site. They'd want to buy souvenirs and trinkets.

The kids would want to stroke and pat and pet the animals, but that wasn't going to happen. These creatures were feral. As a volunteer vet, I had to put my foot down.

Everyone soon realised that this was a no-no on so many levels. Can you imagine? Children running, holding a hand devoid of a couple of fingers or a guy limping on a sandaled foot short of a big toe? It certainly wouldn't wash. It wasn't worth it.

So, the plan went ahead to put in a high, wire fence to keep out the tourists. It was clear, the animals weren't interested in straying from their new habitat. They were content to play in amongst the trees, chase a rabbit or two, pray to their gods at dawn and dusk. A perfect life.

Three times a day, the butcher's van came around for feeding time. Twice a day, a truck rolled up from the local fisheries to throw fish-heads and tails over the fence. Pet shops got involved, bringing dried food and tinned cat and dog food every week. Enough to feed the five thousand!

I helped out with feeding times and looked out for injuries or illnesses to treat, in my capacity as volunteer vet. My job was the easiest. Much easier than my role at the local veterinary practice where we treated sickness and accidents in the hundreds. These ferals seemed to be immune.

I was convinced that Mother Nature and their gods kept a lookout. Who could blame them. The things humans had done over time, dicing with DNA, creating weird species of creatures for power and pleasure; animals putting up with pain so that people could dominate. Mother Nature was coerced into accepting man's dastardly designs in producing bigger apples, straighter bananas, oranges even more orange. Then there was the introduction of dwarfish trees, shorter shrubs, flowers without perfume. You name it. Folks were flush with the fun of playing God.

***

Three years into the 'Mutt-n-Mog Mound' project, there was trouble. The magic of the number three. Ah, there it was!

On a fine, well-visited day, a video appeared on social media, of a cat and two dogs, beyond Mutt-n-Mog Mound, playing in the meadow. They were fighting over a very large liver, a juicy-looking rump steak and a long link of sausages. The headline read:

ANIMALS AT 'MUTT-N-MOG MOUND' ARE EATING PEOPLE

A conspiracy theory if ever there was one. My cats and dogs had no need to hunt and kill people for dinner. The meat was donated by our trusty butcher. He liked to give away the leftovers at the end of his working day. I commented on the video to no avail. I put up a post on Instagram with an explanation. I added a vehement denial.

There were demonstrations outside the fence; protesters carrying placards. Chanting. Although none of it would mean a thing to the cats and dogs inside the fencing (not one of them could read, write or understand human language), the rabble's message was:

GET OUT OR GO VEGAN, YOU ANIMALS! WE'LL KILL YOU, WE'LL CULL YOU!

Still, the stories landed in abundance. I did an interview on North-East News that seemed to do the trick – mostly. My claim to fame! Except that the placard-carrying mob outside, continued their call for a cull of my beloved dogs and cats. Can you believe it? A cull! It didn't work, thanks to the support from local and not-so-local communities. Game over. For the time being, anyhow.

***

Life went on at Pleasantree Woods – pleasantly, you might say. I spent much of my volunteering time at dusk and dawn, communing with my favourite, gnarled old oak tree, surrounded by mutts and moggies of all descriptions. They had become my good friends. Persian and Burmese cats cuddled up and purred loudly on my cross-legged knees. Smiling Huskies salivated and laid-back Labradors leaned over to lick my face. The wizened oak, my World Tree, listened as I whispered. He never spoke with words but communicated wisely, all the same. I asked him if he knew whether "something" was likely to happen in year six – it being a multiple of three (my auspicious number). I was sworn to secrecy when he told me about Odin's ravens, Hugin and Munin. Apparently, the Norse god's birds have powers of prediction. They'd squawked a report as they sat on Odin's shoulders and whispered. In the ninth year of Mutt-n-Mogg Mound there would be a shocking incident. The tree told me nothing more.

* * *

Time rolled forward and I forgot all about that conversation between me and the grand old Oak. Pleasantree's Woodland thrived. The meadow was filled with the scent of wildflowers. And everywhere, cats and dogs from the four corners of the globe (if that's possible) lived a life they had forged by unspoken consent – a hierarchy of kingly and queenly cats, soldierly dogs and the hoi-polloi of mutts and moggies. Some prowled at night, some stalked through the day, all singing (or mewling, or barking) from the same hymn-sheet. All lived off the fat of the land. And their community, such as it was, with leaders and followers, grew like Topsy.

The resident dogs– cute Shih-tzu and Chihuahua puppies included – continued to raid rabbit burrows. No harm done; it was more of a circus and less than a war. Wagging their tails, they smiled their doggy-laughter from beyond the tall fence. The cats – Main Coons, Russian Blues, you name it– sat aloft the trees, looking altogether adorable. They didn't mind the people that visited, as long as they kept their distance. It worked well, enticing the enamoured cat-and-dog lovers to keep up the visits. Hotdogs and burgers sold like the clappers. Ice-creams were scoffed by children, grannies and grandads alike.

***

That ninth year came along as quick as a flash. In July of that year, the north-east - and the whole darn world, for that matter - was treated to a spectacle that would be remembered forever.

It was mid-afternoon, on a warm, blue-skied day. Hardly a cloud in the sky. I wandered toward the Mound to pet the dogs on guard. *Strange,* I thought, *they're not here.* No cats asleep in the hedgerows, either. Not one kitty dozing up a tree. *Where are they all?*

Heading down in the direction of the river, I heard snuffling purrs and yelping "woof-woofs". It was way too early for their usual at-dusk congregation. They were never here until the sun bobbed on the horizon – until today.

I drifted over to the foot of the Tree of Life and patted his trunk. He groaned, huffing and puffing, as though he was in pain. Looking up into his wrinkled old face, I saw that he was fading away into misty vaporous cloud. His branches vanished, his leaves quivered like feathers, fluttering to the ground.

'What's going on?' I asked, watching his lop-sided, twisted smile disappear into the distance. He shimmered like a dimming star. Then he was gone; replaced by a devilishly handsome and haughty grey horse.

What? Baffled, I stepped backward. I noticed the horse rear up on his eight legs. *Eight legs.* I yelled. 'Eight Legs'. That meant something to me. The cats and dogs hissed, growled and screeched too. Terrified. Then I recognised him; remembered him from books I'd read about mythical gods of the Norse lands. I howled his name –

'Sleipnir, is that you?'

He snorted, letting out a languorous "neigh".

The cats and dogs began thumping on the ground with their paws. Rat-a-tat-tat – it sounded like an unearthly drum-roll.

Already agog with excitement, I was doubly so when an enormous giant of a man slipped into Sleipnir's saddle. *It must be Odin.* Not a bit how I imagined him; not the blond, handsome god I expected. This guy was old as the hills but sprightly. Gnarly, he was, and pock-marked around the face like he'd had acne in his youth. His grey hair, tousled with ringlets, matched the colour of his eyes. They sparkled like silver with good humour and kindness – such kindness. I was bowled over. So were the felines and canines: they greeted him as though he was their favourite grandad. They fell over one another in their hurry to climb his hefty legs, scale his muscled shoulders, nuzzle and lick his bearded face.

Odin noticed me when I laughed. Told me who he was. Thanked me for my service.

What?

Told me it was time for them to go soon. Said he was waiting for the bridge to open and they'd be off.

'Ah, here it is,' said Odin, pointing upward to a huge, beautiful rainbow curving above a reddening, setting sun, 'C'mon, everyone. Look lively. Over the Rainbow Bridge we go.'

'Where are you going?' I asked.

'A magical place. Where I live. Where my horse and ravens belong. These cats and dogs too.'

'Will I see them ever again?' I stared at the bridge. I saw hundreds and hundreds of my furry friends, gambol, prance and dance toward its rainbow hues. They couldn't have been happier, pawing at me, lovingly, in passing.

'Nevermore!' Odin's two ravens cackled and cawed.

'Cut it out, birds,' Odin said. And to me, 'Not goodbye, but fare thee well, veterinary lady.'

'Oh!' I felt like crying a river – *my* river at Mutt-n-Mog Mound. I plopped down on the shale in my baggy jeans and striped, blue shirt. I gazed after Odin, Sleipnir, Hugin and Munin.

The tears I shed, led me into stuporous wailing, sobbing for the loss of my felines and canines. They lifted their heads up, proudly worshipping Odin; their future assured, above and beyond the Rainbow Bridge, into the magical Upperworld.

I felt movement in my lap, looking down in surprise. A sleek, black Chantilly cat curled round and around my midriff. A cute white Jack Russell Terrier, a brown splodge daubed over one eye, nuzzled into my hip.

'Hey, you two, you're missing the parade,' I said. The two of them dug in where they sat. I swear they shook their heads.

'You wanna come home with me?' They most definitely nodded their heads in reply.

'C'mon then, guys.' They walked with me until we landed home.

'Who needs myths and gods, eh, boys?' I asked Pitch and Patch (their brand-new adoptive names).

'Your mamma's gonna worship the ground that you walk on.'

QUE SERA, SERA

~

RIDING THE WAVE OF CHANGE

Que Sera, Sera
– Riding the Wave of Change

W ho am I? What am I?

A mantra of mine – "can't ring the phone, can't write a text, can't send an email" - could be an enticing clue to my existence.

Let me give you another. A riddle. I wasn't born – I was minted.

Just in case. I'll give you one more go. I'm inanimate. An object, so they say. Don't let that impact on you. I'm not here to be objectified or vilified. Granted, I haven't got a heart, but I have plenty of soul to go around. Enough for both the heavens and earth.

Perhaps you've guessed it by now. I'll tell you anyway …

I'm a COIN. And not just any old coin. A 1971, ten pence piece. Brought into being in the year decimalisation came to British currency. I'm the common denominator, you could say; the British pound counted in "tens" from that day forth. An Olympic medallist of money.

I stomped into being to the tune of loud rhythmic machinery. The din – clunk click – of the making and shaping of coins. Blinked in sync with the giggling of my tinkling peers, my brothers and sisters -10p's R US!

From the Royal Mint, this huge palace of sharp-angled, art-deco glitz, I intended to become a "Rich Bitch". Live the charmed life of a lucky-coin celebrity. Destined to be a star. Maybe even a superstar. Small in stature - big, so very big, in ambition.

Ambition be beggared! Desire doomed from the outset. Then there was hate in my heart: for the first time ever. What happened? You may well ask. You see, for my debut appearance, I found myself in a dirty mackintosh pocket. I have to say I was alarmed, disgusted by mounds of stringy tobacco looking like a faecal-filled colostomy bag. And shards of mouldy peanut shells pointed like daggers at my retching soul. I was travelling on a messy, litter-strewn, long-distance bus. Rusty, squeaky brakes squealed all the way from Central London to Newcastle-upon-Tyne's city of pits and ships. Ugh – grime. Can't bear being in muck.

The thing is, my having OCD to a lesser or greater extent is a pertinent piece of my personality. I'm a neat freak. I prefer an orderly, organised existence. I detest dirt and dust with a purposeful passion. I admit to being a wipe-it-clean junkie. Sanitary living. And laudable language – swear if you dare.

I heard a cough and a spluttering sneeze as my human carrier alighted the bus at our Newcastle destination. A filthy snot-and mucous-ridden paper hankie was stuffed into his pocket where I'd hidden. Trying to avoid the abyss of a frayed-edged hole to who knows where, I baulked. That's when I activated my powers of prayer and telepathy.

***

I have a clear belief system. It's possible you've heard of "The Champion of the Inanimate" – though possibly not. I've always believed in her, though I've never telepathized with the lady on high. She's way above my pay grade. I'm more prone to communicating with our monetary deity, "The Empress of Any Amount". She's our go-to guru in times of peril. At least, that's what we coins believe she's for. Can't ring her, like I've already told you, though I'm able to talk to her via coin-text. I'm wary of telling you what coin-text is because you probably wouldn't understand. Suffice to say, it's a musical scale of tinkles, clinks and chimes. A vibration of my body against any kind of surface will do the harmonious trick.

So, when I decided to sing my tinkling chant, I was in earnest. I was not meant for this ... this filth! I'm worth so much more. I'm destined for better, more pristine, gleamier things.

Now, I'm no psycho - at least I hope not – though occasionally, I've grasped ...what's that phrase ... the other side of the coin. The tail end rather than the head. "Kill or be Killed" is what I'm thinking. Does that mean I live in an ethical void? Hey, who cares. I'm honourable enough for my own liking.

I'm in such a negative frame of mind. And I'm not the one who wants to be dead. To coin the phrase, "To be or not to be? That is the question," is no dilemma at this point. I certainly couldn't face "BE-ing" right now! Every pore – if I had pores -would be mud-filled with slime.

Granted, when I was in the Mint, I'd spent that sliver of my existence within a silver circle of cleanliness and happiness. Though, for much of this bus-ride, I've been upset, infuriated – downright depressed.

So, my whole being conveyed a message – on the nail for immediate payment - to The Empress of Any Amount: Brr …brr …ring …ring (Just joking! Can't talk on the phone, remember?)

HELLO, EMPRESS. BAD CIRCUMSTANCES. I'M IN THE FILTH. SMITE THIS BUS-LOAD OF FILTHY FOLK. KILL THEM ALL.'

Que sera sera, whatever will be will be, she replied.

'What's that supposed to mean?' I asked her, feeling churlish to say the least. Of course, she couldn't hear me, so I repeated it in capital letters so she got the full might of my disgruntlement.

Exactly that, she said. **Make your own destiny.**

HUH, was my reaction. The Empress had taken not a blind bit of notice of my request. All I wanted – ever *really* wanted – was to be clean. Oh, it would be nice to exist as moneyed money too. But believe me, that would not be paramount. Muck would drive me mad – truly. To the Empress, perhaps, I'm just loose change, jingling about. An aimless unfortunate. A vile un-fragrant vagrant.

* * *

From the station, I landed in a tatty, leatherette satchel, as part-payment for the evening newspaper.

I heard the trains tapping out the 1812 Overture – da-da-da-daa – as I rattled and chinked, side-by-side with the filthiest, tainted coins imaginable. I watched the well-heeled and poorly shod humans, from a peephole in the bag, sauntering, walking, running for connections to destinations. I wished there was a warm, affluent destination for me. Not today, I feared.

Given away as kiddie pocket money, I ended up in the sticky-fingered grip of a child. Oh, lord, now I was clenched in a mangy little fist. I was skipped and hopped toward the sights, smells and atmosphere of Ye Olde Sweetie Shoppe. Lollies, liquorice, aniseed, mint – I could almost taste the candied confections.

I called upon the Empress a second time. Brr … brr … ring…ring. What else could I do?

NB. MADAM EMPRESS. MY CIRCUMSTANCES ARE UNTENABLE. GET ME BEYOND THE GRIP OF THIS SNOTTY-NOSED KID. MAKE HIM SPONTANEOUSLY COMBUST.

All to no avail. Again, she explained in her own inimitable way. Same damnable explanation it was. No change there.

Que sera sera, whatever will be will be. The future's not ours to see ...

* * *

The sweet shop was a deep brown wooden affair with dull, dusty floorboards and shelf upon shelf of tall, glass jars packed tight with edible goodies. Yelling children causing chaos and commotion. I needed to be beyond the knuckles of that slavery-chopped, snotty-nosed kid. Finally, he chose a Mars bar and a Kit-Kat, threw me over the counter toward a moustachioed, grey-haired shopkeeper who promptly kicked me to the filthy floorboards. Obscenely stained, unfit to be seen, I considered I must be sad and angry. I'd gone from shiny to grimy in no time at all. This surely was hell on earth. I was covered in soiled, filthy footprints before I could say 'Chunk o' Change'. My OCD went into overdrive. Into panic-mode.

I tried another lament to the Empress of Any Amount, hoping she wouldn't fail me this time - Brr ... brr ... ring...ring:

'DEAR EMPRESS - THROW ME DOWN THE STAFF TOILET. PULL THE CHAIN. LET ME DRIFT, DOWNWARD AND OUTWARD, GET CLEANSED BY THE SALTY SEA.'

Nope. Not a hope in hell of assistance. Just the same old, same old:

Que sera sera, whatever will be will be.
The future's not ours to see ...

No rescue, despite my agitated messages that jingle, jingle, jingled into space. Nothing. Not even a plump question mark. I felt abandoned.

For all the good the Empress had done me, I may as well have climbed the ladder to the Champion of the Inanimate, greatest goddess of all. Possibly a step too far. To her, it's likely I'm just a lowly metal cheapskate coin.

I suppose I could contact the Lord of Filthy Lucre. One of these days, I might just do that. Turn to the dark side. Jump into the fiery furnace of hell. Turn my back on the light and those coppery pennies from heaven.

I lay on the sweetshop's dirty floorboards for what seemed like years. Turned out it was at least a couple of years, or more. Until the grey-haired old proprietor gave up the business to his daughter.

When she checked around the shop, proposing a makeover of the premises, she found me. My gratitude knew no bounds; until I was rudely grabbed, rubbed and spat on. Then she stuck me in a rusty cash register. Nothing to see. Nothing to do. Endlessly boring, soul-destroying. Anyhow, rust could easily upset all the "joie de vivre" my metallic metabolism was wont to allow. Eventually, I was slung in a brand-new till, lined with sparkling, gleamy metal. Well, I admit I felt a bit more comfortable. Comfortable but stuck. Fervently learning how to be patient – to wait, wait, wait.

***

After a long, laborious while, I was given as change to a man buying toffees and chocolate for a trip to the cinema. He said, 'Interesting,' as he turned me over and over in the palm of his hand, flicked me into the air with nifty thumb and forefinger and kissed me with tender, mint-flavoured lips. I wouldn't have thought I had the capacity to feel love for a human but with this guy, I was getting close. Maybe I was just flattered. He said, 'Hmm – quite a find. You need a clean-up, Miss Ten Pence!' Music to my ears. 'Sort you out when I get you home, little beauty. I'll polish you within an inch of your life.'

His name was Michael. On the way to some posh picture house, he introduced me to his wife and two young daughters, holding me in the palm of his hand. I wanted to shy away until I was clean and fit to be seen but everyone was impressed. Except one of the girls who remarked I was 'sick'. I've never been ill in my whole life, apart from the OCD. *That's* sometimes debilitating and nerve-wracking. Later, I found out, 'sick' means fabulous. Silly me.

I sat behind Michael's ear in the dark cinema, in front of a brightly lit screen, to watch a cartoon movie called, "Cinderella". My new boss had passed over the "readies" to get tickets and I was excited, not knowing anything about movies or cartoons, but having heard that Cinderella is a rags to riches story. *Her* goddess, the fairy godmother, was a great deal more helpful than *my* uncaring goddess. Now I could begin to celebrate my forthcoming good fortune. Not expecting riches, I had a good feeling I would be clean, happy and valued. From in the red - to in the green. From stony broke to cozy living. Fantastic. That'll do for me.

To heck with The Empress. I rang - coin-texted her, pardon me, full of myself. This was my message. Brr … brr … ring…ring:

NB. CHANGE OF FORTUNE. STICK YOUR ASSISTANCE WHERE THE SUN DON'T SHINE, DEAR LOSER EMPRESS.

***

Michael was as good as his word. Clean and shiny, as though newly minted and well-worthy of my acquired glint, I was in my metallic element. He put me to bed in a pristine velvet drawstring bag with six lookalike coins. I was relaxed, happy to share our beautiful boudoir. And I, like my bedfellows, was in awe of my leader and mentor.

He was an insurance broker, weekdays. At weekends, he became 'Micky the Tricky Magician', entertaining silver-spooned children at parties. Apart from his family, it was his greatest love. His happy hobby. What a guy!

We did birthdays in backyards and gardens prettier than picture-postcards. They might have featured on Gardener's World. Rhododendrons in warm pinks and mauves. Fiery-red Virginia creeper, clambering through rambler roses. Lit-up barbeques, essence of charcoal, odours of burgers and hotdogs. Sometimes there were steaks and salmon fillets. I was in awe, not that I needed sustenance. I haven't exactly got a digestive system. We attended Christmas parties in immaculate lounges, all silver and chrome, deep-pile carpets and expensive, pine-scented, tinsel-decorated spruces. Kids with clean-as-a-whistle hands; party frocks of whispering silks and satins; smart, long-trousered suits with white shirts and bow ties. Micky as Santa! Me, as glittery as the angel on top of the Christmas Tree.

Micky would twiddle and twist me through the fingers of his right hand, from index to pinky-finger – and back again, telling jokes, pulling furry toy rabbits from a hat, clever with dexterity. I was sparkling. Queen of Hearts. The Bee's Knees. – Decade after glorious decade. At last, I believed I was in the realms of Legal Tender.

Who needed death or murderous intent when life was sweet – and clean. Not I. As far as I was concerned, fractious old Empress of Any Amount was a matterless, miserable skin-flint – and no longer was I remotely skint.

Until …

***

One dreary, rainy, shopping day, Micky's wife asked for a 10p for the loo. Out I was pulled from my velvet niche. Reluctantly, I might add. I bore Micky no ill-will, him being under the thumb and all. But her, I wished for 'wifey' the most painful death imaginable. I hadn't telepathized for years. Now, I was ready to send an "ultra-high importance" message imploring The Empress to drown Mrs Micky, shove her head down a dirty lavatory in the Ladies. Up and down slowly, agonizingly. TILL DEATH DISAPPEARED HER. How dare she even think about taking away this coin of the realm from an enjoyable life with my Micky.

But before I could "Brr … brr … ring…ring", Wifey shoved me into the metal slot of a graffiti-covered door in the Ladies and I was gone in a flash, into blackness, a dark pit of despair. I coin-texted a "HELP" to my deity without expecting a ring back – or indeed any hope.

And I got none. Not a word. Not even a Que Sera. My elders, gods and betters cared not a hoot or a tinkle.

I belly-flopped into where the rest of the miserable, unclean coins lay. I felt like gagging. Here I was, in a dark, stinking pit of despair. It felt like this might be my final resting place. Gone. Dead to the world in a metal coffin.

Coins pitter-pattered out each time my tomb opened, collected by large, rough fingers.

Not me! I was pushed and pulled about, upside down and sideways. Glued, I became, to the rusty wall inside the tin machine by some well-chewed bubble-gum. I listened, sickened by sounds of farts and sludgy clarts. Dirty, despicable people! I lay there for something like millennia. Incarcerated, clapped-out. Here for eternity. My OCD came back with a vengeance.

I thought about who I could send a begging message too. I was pleasantly surprised to remember the Countess of Currency and the Mage of Moolah. How could I have forgotten about them?

Here goes …

I chinked, chimed and jingled my coin-text to both, knowing that I possessed more importance than any greenback dollar or paper lettuce-leaf, praying with fervour to these financial wizards of lolly and loot to get me out of here. With my celebrity, they should at least listen and respond. Anything except 'Que Sera' would do.

Brr ... brr ... ring...ring. HELP ME, I'M DYING!

I did get a promissory note from the Mage, saying he'd give me assistance if he could.

IT IS UNLIKELY HOWEVER, he messaged. YOU'RE IN THE HANDS OF FATE.

Well ... blooming perfect!

Just before I decided to join the dark demon, desperately dial up the Lord of Filthy Lucre, I heard voices. A boom of rattling and banging sounded on the metal cell I occupied with all the down-and-outs of half-dead dough. I assumed we'd be hauled off to be buried or smelted down into a tin bin of redacted resources.

***

How wrong was I? On the auspicious day, this jaded, faded, degraded monetary being was rescued. Let me tell you, I've never in my life been so pleased to be scratched and scraped. Bubble-gum be gone! I felt ragged fingernails clawing at my front; my belly etched with the queen's face that pouted regally. My back lay against the palm of a rough hand, covering a carved tattoo of my iconic – my very own - fierce lion. What was happening to me? If I was able to move of my own accord, I would have considered fight or flight. There was no need. This was a gentle, lilting, welcome Geordie voice.

'Eeeh! See this, Mabel. Stuck to some gum. Look, t'other side is still a bit shiny. Come an' look, Billy.'

Another voice spoke up, deep, drawling and Scottish. 'Hmm, a wee ten pence. 1971. Might be worth a bob or two. My lad collects coins. Och, d'you mind if I tek it away off hame?'

'Why, aye, get yersel' away. I'll get shot o' this lot.' She pointed at the warped metal coin I'd been rescued from. 'See yer the morrow. We'll install the card reader in the morning.'

I felt the sun on my grimy face and the heat from the large hand I was passed along to. I was exhausted. I was grateful. I wanted a wash and clean-up more than any time in my whole existence. I could only hope …

* * *

'C'mon, wean. Let's git oan wi'it.' Billy spoke in a dialect I hardly understood. But I got the gist when he opened his wallet. Placed me inside. Threw me onto a plush seat. Drove his van. Home, I thought. Home was where Micky lived. Are there other places called Home?

There sure were. Billy carried me into a semi-detached house in a place called Wideopen. And it certainly was a spacious sort of abode with lots of rooms.

He shouted out, 'Danny', as he ran upstairs – and upstairs again to more rooms. 'Come 'n take a wee look, son.' A thatch of red hair greeted us from a door leading to an attic space.

'What, Dad?'

Tall, bald-headed Billy showed me to Danny. I really thought he might say 'Ugh' at the state of me.

He didn't. He said, 'Wow!'

Then he said, 'Let's get you freshened up, little coin. Thanks Dad, I'll need a new mount for this one. Pride of place once I get her sorted.'

Get on with it, I thought. Put me in a bathtub and scrub me clean and dry.

Much to my delight, Danny did just that. My bathtub was plastic, big enough for me with room to spare. He pushed a button on the side.

Oh, my, it was a whirlpool. Batteries included. Just the job.

I sank to the bottom, more than willing to be swirled around in bubbles of delightful sweet-smelling cleaning stuff. I fancied I was with the money-angels in a heaven of soapy suds. Didn't want to move – ever. Amen to that.

Once out of the bath, I was wrapped in a soft gown and handled with white gloves. Danny rubbed me gently with oils, lotions and potions that had me sighing with relief. No more aches and pains. Not a worry in the world.

'There you are,' said Danny, whipping off his dusty, damp gloves, chucking them aside.

'Clean as a whistle and silvery as the moon, you are, Ten.' That's what he calls me. Nice little nickname, don't you think?

Nowadays, I lounge about, living in luxury. Mounted on a queenly throne, set in a gilded frame. Wallowing on a raised chaise. Rich beyond compare.

Dan whispers to me, 'In another fifty years, Ten, you'll be antique: Priceless. Worth a fortune.'

And here I shine, cossetted by this nice young fellow who rewards me, on my plush cushion, daily, with feather dusters. I'm framed in splendid style. I'm cleaner, much cleaner, than I've ever been.

I'm revered like I'm some sort of superstar. Dan's dad, Billy, is my super-hero – 'Dan the Man' is my new-found idol.

**

Suddenly, I'm incensed. There, up on high, on hallowed ground, sit my very own coin-goddesses, who left me to my fate. Refused to give a helping hand on the road to my destiny.

Thanks for nothing, I think. For not caring a pennyworth. Left to my fate. The Hand of God? Hah! If I had the power, I'd raze those pseudo deities to blazes.

I'd travelled alone. Nobody gave a toss for this ten pence piece. From Mint to Skint. Glitz to Blitz. Buried like the Dead. Uncovered … Discovered.

I ring up, Brr … brr … ring…ring, sending a message, a round robin, to these so-called goddesses on high:

About me -

I'm pristine – got DERRING-DO,
Cleanliness *is* Godliness - you know it's TRUE.
No FURTHER correspondence - Not WITH YOU!

**

You know, there's a saying that applies directly to me and my existence, all you followers of my whole existence:

Change is hard at first, messy in the middle and gorgeous at the end.
Yes it is …

A
SNAKE
IN THE
GRASS

A Snake in the Grass

'Settle down, children,' said newly qualified primary schoolteacher, Mister King. 'Year Two begins. I'll take the register first. You know the drill.'

As the seven-year-olds began to chant their names out loud, one-by-one, row-by-row, Mister King took stock of the whole class.

On his first day, the staff room had been full of gossip about one particular child.

'Watch him,' one said. 'Right little psychopath,' said another. 'Wrong-un,' and 'snake-in-the-grass' seemed to be the teachers' general consensus of opinion.

It didn't take long for Mister King to identify the "snake". Within seconds, he was shuddering as he made eye contact with Montague Priorson. The boy's eyes held and terrified his teacher. Unblinking, yet glittering. Tiny, shiny, black as jet. Magnetic, like a bad mood.

The boy leaned forward over his desk, narrow shoulders meeting an almost non-existent neck, belling out to a flat, rounded shovel of a head. A wide, lipless, hypnotic mouth smiled through a forked tongue.

When it was Montague's turn, he half-whispered his name in a quiet-but-ominous way.

'Montague Priorson, sir.'

Only there was something about his speech. Spitting his name out in a languid, lisping hiss, he'd drawled,

'Mon–th -agoo Prior-tthhhh-on, ttthhhh-ir'

According to the tittle-tattle in the staff room, at the tender age of three, Montague had bitten the end of his tongue, in a raging tantrum. Split it right down the middle. Fortunately for him, he'd been given the toy he'd screamed blue murder for, so further damage avoided. Unfortunately, for the community, his behaviour set the trend for his anti-social behaviour.

'Ah,' Mister King said, gulping back his shock at the kid's sinister look. 'Do you use your long name, Montague? Or your short name, Monty?'

'Short, sir.' Monty's forked tongue flickered out as he spoke, giving the impression of a snake; the lisp in his words adding to the unintended imitation. 'Ttthhh-ort.'

The teacher's mouth curved upward in a semi-smirk. It was ridiculous that a seven-year-old lad could create such trepidation in a grown man. Yet the teacher folded his arms as though he was protecting himself.

Try humour thought Mister King. *That'll do it.*

His reply – his snide outburst – had nought to do with Monty's lisp. A fair percentage of the population have a speech impediment of one sort or another. No, what he came out with was more to do with Monty's snake-like appearance. His serpentine, slow and languid hiss. At the end of each sentence and certain words, Monty spat an elongated, yellow-green drool down his almost chinless face. It spooked Mr King no end.

'Sounds to me like maybe you're really "Monty Python".' And he raised an eyebrow; laughed a sort of guffaw.

The whole class giggled, tittered uneasily, glanced sideways at Monty. Perhaps it even struck a chord with them. After all, "the snake" was Monty's nickname. Among the more astute, they called him "snake in the grass". Or so Mr King had heard on the staffroom grapevine.

**

Monty was what you'd call a sneaky kid. Slithered up against fences in the yard. Listening. Glided around doorways. Eavesdropping. Slid around corners. Snooping. Took money with menaces. Allegedly. Monty collected pupils' murmured secrets to gain himself a sandwich here, a packet of crisps there. A fistful of kids' pocket money to keep confidences. 'Or I'll grass!'

**

Mister King, somewhat cowed by his own sarcastic outburst, apologised to the poor, uncomfortable lad. Monty wriggled and rolled in his chair. Truth be told, he was infused with anger. His forehead further flattened, Neanderthal-like; his wide apart slits-for-eyes glistened in tearful resentment. His neck appeared and disappeared into his shoulder-blades as he squirmed, hips undulating, rising upward, then sideways, in reptilian motion.

Noticeably bigger and taller than the rest of the class, he slowly stood, curling an ankle around his chair. Sent it reeling backward. Monty opened the lengthy slit of his mouth and spat.

'Monty Python?' he seethed. 'Who's that? Who the *hell* is that, eh? Gonna tell ma and da on you. And my sisters. (Sisters sounded like "thhh-ittthht-ertthh".) You takin' the Micky?'

The children went silent. The room was hushed. The teacher yelled, 'Enough, Monty. 'Sit down, please.'

But it was too late. Monty coiled spring-like. As if a whipcrack had sounded, his whole body became a pointed arrow. Quick as a dart, he was through the door, with a headfirst slither. All he left behind was a fading shadow as he snake-hipped his way, low-to-the-ground, down the corridor.

Afterward – after the whole debacle – after what would occur later - he was to hope he wasn't the cause of the chain of reaction; the events that were yet to happen.

***

'OK, children. Early playtime today. Off you go.' Trying to think on his feet, Mister King chose the worst of bad options and ran after Monty. Couldn't spot him anywhere. Not anywhere in the L-shaped corridor.

Ah, well, he thought. *This'll surely upset Miss Spoke, the headmistress. But needs must. I'd better report it.*

He turned the corner toward Miss Spoke's office and landed slap-bang on the tiled floor. Whumph!

Dark eyes glinting, hinting malice, Monty had hurled himself at Mister King. Curled himself around the teacher's left leg, up and up – squeezing, crushing, biting his opponent's meaty thigh. Mister King stared down at his leg, disbelieving. The child's mouth had opened so wide, his jaw seemed to dislocate as he snapped off a chunk of gristle - and his teacher's trouser-leg. Chewing. Dribbling. Spitting in a hissy-fit.

'Ugh. Nasty,' (Na-ttth-tty)

Sliding further up, twisting around a sinewy neck, reaching his teacher's handsome face – Monty nutted Mister King's nose. Blood spurted into Monty's curve-toothed, evil smile.

'Nexthhht time, I'll crushsh you. Ttthhwallow you up in one go.'

Looking up into those cruel features and forked tongue, the teacher gasped.

'Don't like "Monty Python". Seen him on the TV. Silly men doing daft things. But I found a python picture on my phone. I *like* him.' Monty paused, tapped his mobile phone. A whispered whistle emitted from between sharp, arching teeth. 'I *really* like him. Lottthhh.'

'AND DON'T EVER, NEVER, LAUGH AT ME, TTH-TH-IR' Split-tongue-between-teeth, Monty stammered, spat and hissed. 'I AM THE PYTH-TH-ON.'

Monty slip-slid his feet, side-to-side down the corridor, like he was on a slalom-run. With legs bent at the knee, his lower limbs struck a rhythmical, wriggling beat.

Jeez - thought Teacher. He *looks* like a python. A slick, smooth snake of a lad!

'Goin' home now. Out of my way...TH-TH-IRRR.'

Monty smacked into his teacher's kidneys with a bony fist. All Mr King could do was curl up into a foetus on the floor.

***

The teacher picked himself up, groaning. Knocked heavily on Miss Spoke's door.

'Ah, come in, Mister King,' she called, 'No "MIST-A-KING" that knock, pardon the pun.' She laughed.

Mr King said, 'Hah,' with a sarcastic Elvis-sneer of his upper lip.

'Lighten up, Joe.'

'Huh.'

'Only "JOE-KING". Pardon that one too.'

'MIS-SPOKE again, I see?' Mister King retaliated.

'Touché. My, my, look at your face. And there's blood on your trousers. What happened?'

Joe told Miss Spoke about his wrestling bout with Montague Priorson.

She laughed. 'Tit for Tat, I reckon, Joe.'

Joe thought Miss Spoke was being unprofessional. Then again, his own conduct in the classroom had been childish to say the least.

He changed the subject and asked, 'Are Social Services involved in this lad's welfare? Behaviour seems off the charts.'

'Yeah, they keep an eye. Joe, go see the school nurse, get cleaned up. Take the day. Get me your scheme of work. I'll oversee Year Two, for the rest of their classes today.'

'You know,' she added, 'this village was just another sleepy backwater. But since the Priorson family moved here, well … And Joe, that kid tried, not long ago, to separate his tongue further down the middle. Said it would give him a better "hiss". Used a penknife. The knife dad cuts his dope with. His sisters stopped him. Just in time.'

Joe gagged, felt like vomiting. Limped off to Reception. He needed to collect some lesson plans and schemes of work for Miss Spoke. And he needed Monty's notes for himself. Research on the kid and his folks – that's what he needed most of all.

He wanted to see Monty's people for himself. Try to understand the family dynamic. Maybe try to help, somehow.

* * *

It took Joe a little under an hour to hobble from school to Monty's house. Passing a slagheap on his left, he scaled several grassy slopes toward a steep, shale clifftop on his right. Limped through a days-gone-by pit village, Pitslaggen by the Cliffs. Seemed about as dangerous as box of kittens, though there was an underlying atmosphere of threat too. Where did that come from? Was it all about the Priorson family, as Miss Spoke had insinuated? Surely not.

Joe read some of the notes he'd borrowed from school. Details about Monty. Records about Monty's twin sisters. He was seven; they were sixteen. Monty had always been difficult. Hard to please. Ma and da pandered to him. One quote from a social worker – 'He gets away with murder'. *A bit steep*, thought Joe. It also seemed that Social Services were rarely let into the family home. And if they were, there was no information. No cooperation. "Just a hiss and a glob of spit from Monty's mouth," – phrased in speech-marks no less! Most peculiar. Phrases like *budding sociopath*. Words like *on the spectrum. Way off the spectrum!* A child psychologist's report said Monty required counselling. Warranted therapy. Of what kind, nobody seemed sure.

'Well, well,' Joe said, aloud. 'What a muddle.'

He lame-legged his way up a tarmac path toward the gravelled clifftop, through a worse-for-wear gate and knocked.

'Who's there?' shouted a female voice, chafed and throaty; a smoker's gravelly tone.

'Mister King, Monty's teacher.'

'Gerraway. Gann on.'

'I come in peace, Missus Priorson.'

'Alreet then.'

***

Her back was to him as she waddled duck-like to a threadbare, bobbled sofa. Threw her short, podgy, shell-suited self into its creaky springs.

Joe noticed a bong, overturned on dirty lino. A half-empty bottle of cheap vodka clinked beside it.

'Whaddya want?' Dad Priorson glared in a parody of Dead-Eye Dick. Hairy-chested, scratching an armpit under a filthy string vest. He adjusted the crotch of his grey-black joggers with a stupid, "pleased-with-himself" grin.

'Monty's the spitting image of you,' Joe blurted. 'Around the eyes, especially.'

'Snake-eyes, yeah? I get it all the time. Mind you, our lad thinks *he's* a bloody snake since you opened yer gob, Mister.'

'Aye, Monty-bleedin-Python, you called 'im' Ma broke in. 'Make 'im a cuppa, you two Jellies, I'm smoking a fag.'

'Who's you two Jellies",' Joe asked. Then, turning, he saw two look-alike teenagers behind him at the kitchen doorway.

'Jellybean n Jellytot, the twins,' Da butted in, coughing as he sucked happily on a spliff, stinking out the whole room.

'That their real names or nicknames?' Joe wanted to know, waving away the smoke from under his nose.

'Real, o' 'course. And why the hell not? You got a problem with my lasses' names?'

Joe observed two black eyes. One each for the pretty, diminutive young ladies.

Shaking his head slowly, he pointed – and said, 'And what happened here?'

'Monty done it.' Ma sniggered. 'Wanted the girls to back him up. All that palaver in the classroom.'

She turned on the girls. 'Didn't back him, did you? Did you, Jellybean?'

'No, Ma. Anyway, it wasn't just black eyes. Kicked us in the shins today, walking him to school.'

'Aye, right.' Ma turned back to Joe. 'Now 'e wants a daft camouflage soldier suit. To look like one o' them dislocated pythons you told 'im about.'

'Reticulated,' corrected Joe.

'Yeah, well, that an'all. I've 'ad to get 'is camouflage thingy same day delivery. Bashed me, 'e did, till I said OK. He's a good kid, though, poor lad. Apple of his da's eye.'

'Poor girls, more like,' said Joe. Was he putting his foot right in the snake pit? 'Got some Arnica for those bruises?'

''s OK, I'll get that cuppa tea.' Said Jellybean. Or was it Jelly tot?

What sort of names were these, Joe thought. Moronic. I blame the parents. They're the culprits in all this mess.

'No girls, it's fine,' Joe smiled pleasantly. 'Need to see Monty. Where is he?'

'He's there, up the cliff.'

***

Joe traipsed upward, climbing a steep slope, feeling the pull on his injured leg.

He watched Monty writhe a meandering zigzag on his belly on the clifftop.

Practicing, Joe supposed. Python stuff. *Is it me and my big mouth? Or is it the parents' pandering to Monty's whims?*

In his best teacher-voice, Joe jumped straight in, 'You know, Monty, snakes can be kind and caring. They don't need to hit their mums and dads; give their sisters black eyes. Doctors, psychologists – even vets - have pole-climbing snakes as their slogans. Do some good. Do no harm.'

'Bollocks,' was Monty's answer, 'What about Basilisk?' (Ba-tthh-ili-tthhhkk) 'He's King of Snakes and kills just by looking at you. Looked him up on the 'net. He's who I'm gonna be when I grow up. Gonna be a gang leader. Gonna be a drug dealer. Sick, eh?'

Joe King was at a loss. He sighed. Shrugged his shoulders. Said, 'Sick is right.' He couldn't help himself.' Sickening is even more correct.'

Monty laughed heartily, as though he might like his strange new teacher after all.

Joe waved a farewell, setting off down the hill, punching some numbers on his phone. He alerted Social Services. They assured him someone would visit the Priorson family, next morning.

'Tomorrow morning? Not straightaway? Well then, sod you, very much.'

The twins met him halfway up the hill, running, breathless. 'Help us out here, Mister King. We're sick of this. Slaves to Da and Ma and Monty. "Clean the house or Monty'll bash ya. Make breakfast, make dinner – or Monty'll crack yer heads together." He'll end up killing us. An' it'll be their fault.'

Joe told them not to worry. Told them Child Services were coming.

'Yeah, right. They'll not get past the front door, betchya,' said Jellytot. Or Jellybean.

They looked to be at their wits' end. They gaped at him from deep, dark pools of large, terrified, round eyes. Pleaded with him from solemn pixie faces; pointed chins.

They look like a pair of little meerkats, thought Joe. Two cute, weaselly little mongooses. Might be the antidote to Monty's python!

'Tell you what?' said Joe. 'How about you play a game with him of snakes and mongooses?'

He told them the Rudyard Kipling story about Riki Tiki Tavi, the grey mongoose who fought – and won - against snakes. About how *they* could win – keep winning - against Monty.

After swapping mobile details with Mister King, they said, 'Wow.' And sped off, skipping like delighted children.

Joe turned and spotted Monty. The boy gazed open-mouthed as though he'd heard every word of Riki Tiki Tavi. His forked tongue, flicking and shifting in the noonday sunshine, his whole body twisted to and fro with inferred warped sarcasm. Even though Monty would have no idea what any of the story actually meant, there was no way he'd heard. No way, unless he had preternatural powers. No way. Joe could think of several words to describe Monty - Cold. Callous, Caustic. Snake-in-the-Grass - but Joe couldn't believe the boy would have some sort of auditory-sensory mystique – could he?

***

Joe King made his way home, nursing his smashed-up nose and painful, bleeding thigh. Next morning, Joe turned on the television, to catch the Northeast news. Whilst washing, shaving, tending wounds, he overheard the name Pitslaggen by the Cliffs. He turned up the volume.

Early this morning, police were called to a bloodbath in the sleepy village of Pitslaggen by the Cliffs in Northumberland. Mr and Mrs Priorson were found dead in their cliffside house, having been assaulted by copious, deadly knife wounds. Twin daughters, sixteen, are both missing. The Priorson's seven-year-old son, rope-bound and dressed in camouflage tracksuit, floated in the sea at the cliff-foot.

Revived by CPR at the scene, onlookers were amazed to hear him screaming, 'MA. DA. KNIFED. HAH! SISTERS. HUH! BIT. SWALLOWED. 'TWAS I, BASILISK – KING OF SNAKES'.

Joe King thought, *Was it my fault? What has Monty done? Are the twins alive? What have they done? Social Services, the police, the press – they'll have a field day. As for Mum and Dad – I have no sympathy.*

Such a conundrum. He wondered whether his telling of the mongoose story had alerted the twins to their newly perceived powers. Had they been the perpetrators? Oh my, had Joe given them ideas that led them to matricide and patricide? Not impossible. Improbable?

Oh my god, I hope not. I hope those girls are innocent. Or are they better alive and guilty?

They're certainly guilty of tying Monty up and throwing him in the drink. At MY behest.

He tried the twins' mobile numbers, several times. Each time, he got voicemail. He left a text: WERE YOU THE ONES WHO USED THE KNIFE? SOLUTION. BLAME MONTY. YOU DON'T NEED SUFFER ANY FURTHER. DELETE THIS MESSAGE IMMEDIATELY. STAY SAFE.

Then he inadvertently mimicked Monty's '*hiss*", in the way of 'Kaa', Jungle Book's sleazy rock python. *Could Monty's snake-obsessions be contagious? Or infectious? Please – NO!*

My Father's Tweed Suit

My Father's Tweed Suit

I sat there, all hunched up, on the floor beside his empty bed, weeping, fingers clutching the old-fashioned quilted bedspread. I was surprised to find myself in what had been my father's bedroom.

Why am I not in my own room, tucked up in my own bed? And why am I crying so hard?

Two bluebottles buzzed around the bronze figurine lamp like moths drawn to the light, full of busy. They chattered gleefully, wings slapping against the heat of the bulb. I heard the sounds of jubilant giggles as their wings were seared, ripped and torn off. I heard them clear as a bell. They seemed to sigh in happy satisfaction as they died on the bedside cabinet.

Get a grip, I told myself. *Suicidal bluebottles, for god's sake?*

I yelled out loud, clawing at my cheeks, ridding myself of the powdery dust that landed on my face; settled on my eyelids.

***

Shaking and sweating, I woke up in my own bed, tucked up safely in my own bedroom, in my own little cottage.

What a strange dream. A dream that involved him? Or his house? My father has been dead a year now. And his house is sold.

There was no love lost between my father and me. Even after his death, I couldn't pretend he was ever my favourite person.

I haven't mourned him, not once – so why? It must be those cheese sandwiches I had for supper with a hefty dose of 'Britain's got Talent' on the telly. Cheese always gives me hellish nightmares. 'No more cheese for you at bedtime young lady!' That's what Mum used to say when I was a kid. I can almost hear her saying it now.

I smiled as I remembered her with the warmth she deserved. My cheerful, chirpy, selfless mum. Not like my dad – my controlling, humourless, philandering dad.

I'll switch the light off - get some proper sleep. Get these thoughts out of my head.

I turned toward my girly-pink bedside lamp, my eyes settling on two dead bluebottles on the shiny surface of the bedside table. That's when I realised it wasn't a nightmare I'd been in the middle of. It was true, after all. I must have been wide-awake when I'd seen those crazy bluebottles laughing, then lifeless, stiff with rigor mortis. Only difference was, they were on *my* bedside cabinet, not Dad's.

As sure as apples are apples, they're dead.

I poked at their stiff-as-cardboard bodies and knew, for sure, they were real.

Suddenly, as if to remind me that something strange was happening, an unearthly voice said in the loudest, demanding tones:

C'MON BLUEBOTTLES, YOUR WORK IS DONE. HOME, SWEET HOME! HELL IS WHERE THE HEART IS!

I don't know if that deep-toned ethereal voice came from the room or inside my head – but it was there, somewhere. I was sure of it.

Then I saw the shadows: deep, dark, cloudy outlines that emerged in slow, eerie motion from the bedroom door, sliding with stealth toward me. Startled, I jumped beneath my bedclothes, whimpering as the amoeba-like silhouette crossed the ill-lit bedroom. I watched its pseudopods sweep up the corpses of the two bluebottles and glide toward me.

I heard a soft wraithlike voice calling my name. KA---T----IE...

***

I watched, terrified, eyes wide-open, as the creature's grey, finger-like wisps floated ever nearer: felt its otherworldly fist curl up around my chin. Tap - Tap - Tapping with a clawed thumb.

Oh, God, this can't be happening. What the hell is this?
And once more … KA---T----IE...

I stiffened, raised a brave hand to slap this spectral shadow-creature into oblivion and felt something grip my elbow. Something razor-sharp settled against my neck, like a shard of glass slicing into my jugular. Then it – whatever IT was - was inside me, marauding, like it was trying to steal my body, assault my mind.

'Stop it!' I yelled. It let go of my arm. I thought I'd won the tussle until I realised it had no need to restrain me. Not now it was in me.

I shoved the palm of my hand against my torn neck, dripping with sticky blood, "What the hell are you doing? Just leave me alone!" My voice squeaked, high-pitched with fear and disgust.

If I was on the set of a horror movie, someone would be shouting, "Cut" by now. But, of course, nobody shouted. Looked like I was on my own.

I started to cry, just like in my nightmare, gripping onto the duvet. I prayed the coolness of the cotton would ease the heat of the entity that had invaded me. I hoped the cover's pristine whiteness would save me from the black thoughts rolling around in my head: lust and hatred, desire and loathing.

Jesus, whose thoughts are these? Not mine! I covered my eyes with my hand. *Are these the thoughts of the thing inside me? Got to fight it Katie...Fight, girl!*

I felt as though I was burning, the thing inside me coursing through every floating red corpuscle of my blood.

Hot! Hot!

It was nestling in my brain, this thing that terrorized me; petrified me to the core.

KA--T----IE...

As it gained control, inch by inch, I could feel myself getting weaker, weaker...I grew faint. I felt as though I was imprisoned. Stuck in some sort of padded cell within my brain. This vile monster had pushed me in here and locked the door tight shut.

It's starting to take me over – but I want it gone. Get out!

In panic, I screamed, "Give me my mind back! Get out! Get out of me!"

I screamed again.

* * *

I rushed to the wardrobe, walking with staccato steps, arms in front of me, stiff like a robot. It didn't care. There was no sympathy. No empathy.

I'm like a puppet on a bloody string. In its grip now.

My body wasn't my own. A stronger presence than me had emerged. Dumbfounded and helpless in that locked cell in my mind, I did its bidding. I tried to fight, but gnarled, gruesome fingers closed over my nerve endings. At every attempt, I was unable to move of my own free will.

What the hell is this thing? A ghoul? A demon? What are you?

My hands moved quickly across the wardrobe's rail until they found what they sought - my father's tweed suit.

My father's tweed suit? What does it want this bloody old moth-eaten suit for? It's been wrapped up and zipped in plastic since he's been gone. Chucked to the back of the wardrobe. His favourite suit. But why would I keep it? Ah, my mum loved that suit. That's why. My lovely, gullible mother.

I felt possessed to don it: wear it like my father had – smart and buttoned-up. Navy tie with a Windsor knot. It was as though my life depended on it. Gripped in a monster's thrall, a ghostly ogre's lair.

***

The suit was too baggy and too long. I laughed at my reflection, gaping at that woman who wore it. It was me, yes…but was it, really? I recognised the ink-black hair with the blue streaks. I'd worn it like that since I'd turned thirty – my claim to youth, I think.

I recognised the slim physique and the long, heavily-ringed fingers. I recognised the high cheek bones, inherited from my mum. Yet none of it seemed familiar: none of it, save the hazel eyes with the day-glow green flecks, care of my depraved deceased father.

What has my father got to do with this debacle? Am I in the middle of this fiasco because of him?

As I looked through the mirror from the dark recesses of my mind – and saw my father's daughter in that suit, I snapped. I remembered what Mum never knew: that it was his 'suit for the ladies' - his 'pulling' suit.

He never even took flowers to the grave. Didn't care when she was alive – cared less when she was dead. Bastard! My mother deserved better than you! I hate you – even dead, I hate you!

I tried to smash the mirror. My fist lashed out but that thing inside me stopped me with tremendous force and nearly broke my arm.

***

QUICKLY, KATIE, TO THE CHURCH – HURRY! That voice in my head jarred every nerve. Was it my father's voice? Whoever's voice, it was a hateful voice and it sent me crazy. I struggled inside the straitjacket of my mind.

'My Italian blood, honey," I remembered my father saying, many years ago now, when I'd challenged him about his unfaithful ways. He'd looked so proud of himself.

I was just a kid, for God's sake!

Maybe he'd got his come-uppance when I cared nothing about his passing. I hadn't shed a tear – not one.

MUST GET GOING, KATIE: GET ME TO THE CHURCH ON TIME.

What church? I never go to church.

Nevertheless, I pulled on high spike-heeled boots to avoid falling over Dad's tweed trouser turn-ups and a thick, silver-spiked leather belt to hold the suit pants up.

This monster must care about keeping my body and soul together, I suppose.

I almost laughed as I tackled the stairs two at a time, wearing not a stitch bar the suit, the tie, the boots, the belt.

Why am I wearing Dad's suit? Is it you in my mind, Dad? This is your doing, I know it, you bastard! But how?

The demon inside, urged me to leave the house at top speed. I twisted my ankle in my top-dollar boots on the staircase - but that "thing" inside me wouldn't let me rest. I was up again, staggering over the threshold in haste, slamming the door behind me.

I felt a rush of cold air that made me gasp.

Look at me, out in freezing temperatures in my father's tweed suit, his vile voice resonating in my head.

My whole body shook.

Maybe it's not him? How could it be him?

Of course it could be him, that arrogant man who betrayed my mum with conquests young enough to be his daughters: lovers my age or younger, dipping into black magic with at least one of them.

***

'The dark arts, honey,' he'd said to me one day when I found a witchcraft book in the garage, 'More exciting than white magic!' He'd laughed, all hale and hearty.

Slithering creep!

My mind settled on a memory of one of Dad's old flames, not much more than a girl – a Goth, dressed in black, looking dazzling - a dabbler in the Satanic arts.

What made me think of her? She'd called herself a witch, the silly cow... Kimberley, that's what she was called... turned up at his funeral with a black rose in her hair...spider's web tattoo on her cheek... spider's web gloves to match ... stupid bitch ...

I lay there in my locked prison cell, banged up in the darkest recess of my mind, with the kind of hatred I hated to see in others. Vindictive hatred.

* * *

I kept on walking, with robotic gait, unable to stop this thing inside me from doing its worst.

Can't stop it. It's strong. Whatever it is, it's too strong.

The suit was itchy: it itched until I had to scratch. I scratched until I drew blood, until the ghoul's stealthy fingers stopped me. I stared at the blood on my hand, trying to comprehend this dark shadow that meandered in my veins and attacked my mind. I hated it with a vengeance.

If you've had a part in this, Dad, I hate you more than ever.

* * *

I took my thoughts off somewhere removed from here, away from the monster controlling my mind.

I remembered Dad's funeral and that feeling of deep, solid darkness in the church that had chilled me to the bone. I remembered hearing my lace-hemmed black petticoats rustle as my knees knocked, thighs shivered and ankles gave way in trembling anger – not at his passing, but at his living.

I remembered sensing ice in my veins as I stalked away from old flame after old flame. All these women who'd had the gall to turn up to eat my ham sandwiches and drink my whiskey at his funeral tea. I was furious. I was overcome with sadness for my hard-done-by mum. Relieved, in a way, that she had succumbed to Alzheimer's disease; that she had no clue about her husband's dalliances with girls young enough to be his daughter.

I have truly detested the sound of rustling lace ever since the day of his burial.

**

The churchyard was still. Nothing dared move in my presence. Something evil was inside me.

The church door creaked open: a beautiful door, shaped like an arch, in thick, noble oak. It gleamed eerily in the moonlight. An owl hooted as though it was taking part in a *Hammer House of Horrors* movie.

"To-whit to-whoo!"

I squeezed my bladder tight shut; I was close to wetting myself in fear.

I took two steps forward over the threshold before the door slammed shut behind me. Pushing my shoulders back, trying hard to look nonchalant, I strolled up the aisle. My steps faltered. I froze as I glanced down at my hands. I was clutching two black candlesticks in either fist. They flew from my fingers, landing in shiny gold candelabra that stood either side of the pulpit - and flickered into flame.

**

'Hello, Guiseppe,' said Kimberley, stepping from behind the shadows of the pulpit.

AH, KIMBERLEY, MY LOVE. YOU LOOK A TREAT IN TAFFETA. It was my father's voice, I was sure, that said those words.

I'm speaking in Dad's voice, for crying out loud! I'm a stand-in at my dead dad's wedding. This is a damned charade and I can't do anything to stop it...

I curled up, locked in my dark chamber, wishing I could be rendered unconscious.

Don't want to be part of this fiasco.

'I've come for you, darling Gus, like I said I would,' cooed Kimberley. 'I summoned you. Aren't I the clever one? Remember how we practised? I've cast a spell through your daughter. Katie was such an easy target – so susceptible. I sent Kobal, Grand Demon of Hilarity and Leonard, Master of Black Magic and Sorcery in the guise of bluebottles. They sent her into a trance-state, cajoled her till she let your spirit in.'

Trance? Let my father's spirit control me? Bitch...I'll bloody kill her...

But I was shattered, no fight left in me.

DO NOT WORRY, MY DEAREST. My father spoke in his strong, masculine voice - through my mouth. I could feel it open and close, tongue against my teeth. I could not bear the revulsion I felt. His words echoed around the prison cell in my head.

KATIE WILL FORGET.

*No, I bloody won't...I'll make myself remember...*I struggled to stay alert now: blinked to stay focussed. I felt my father blink too.

Ah! I was keen to understand I was steeling myself to get into fighting mode. *Keep it up, Katie. Your anger is making you stronger.*

'We must marry, Gus darling, so that I can summon you direct. So that we need never be lonely. What with you dead and me still in the world, this is how we can be together.'

She grasped what she took to be my father's wrists. Yet it was I who pushed her away, letting them know that I, Katie, was still here. I pushed and pushed...

Push her, Katie. Push her away. It's working...I'm getting stronger. Fight, Katie.

Kimberley grasped my wrist again but this time I seemed to be defenceless. Kimberley and my father clasped hands and stared into one another's eyes. Those striking violet eyes of hers mesmerised my father: I could feel his passion rising in my chest; feel his eyes (*my eyes*) glaze over with lust. I felt sick.

'I summoned Azaziel and Baal." Kimberley went on, using Satanic names that repulsed me. 'Baal was the one who came through for us, my love. He will marry us tonight.' They held each other close. My father's arms wrapped themselves around Kimberley's slender waist.

Not Dad's arms, my arms.

The power of my fury gave me some control of my actions. I threw her to the floor.

She picked herself up, snarling, her beauty changing into something unspeakably ugly. But she was no demon: only a misguided fool of a witch who loved my ridiculous father.

My father helped her to her feet and, though he spoke no words, told me to behave myself. I was livid with rage. My emotions fired me up, spurred me on.

'I won't behave, you bastard," I screamed at my father.

My own voice is back! Maybe I can win! Maybe I can fight them!

* * *

It all seemed a little late to strike venom at these two preposterous figures: me in my father's tweed suit and spike-heeled boots and Kimberley with her violet eyes and her black taffeta wedding gown.

I'd made a mistake – a big mistake – in believing I had the better of them.

Because suddenly, she spat out expletives in the vilest language: expletives summoning up Baal. And I wasn't equipped to take action against this vile demon.

Kimberley's saliva sparked gory green flames from a gigantic gold, glazed, two-handled cup as it swirled around the couple as they knelt before Baal.

The flames turned red above the shape of a malformed body and became enormous, oriental crimson eyes that sifted through my brain and found me, pinning me down, flat against the hard floor of the locked compartment of my mind.

I gasped – my father too - but I gasped in pain and rage whilst my father seemed to gasp in awe of this hideous monster.

'Do you Guiseppe Marco Figaro take this woman to be your lawful wedded wife?' Baal smiled as only a demon could. I retched, but my mouth moved to allow my father's deep-voiced:

I DO.

'Do you, Kimberley Jane Clarkson, take this man to be your lawfully wedded husband?'

I do,' responded the taffeta-gowned girl standing before me, gazing into my father's eyes *(my eyes)* with love.

Oh, my god – I'm feeling nauseous again.

'Then I pronounce you man and wife.'

***

Resentment and hatred welled up in me like never, ever before. I pulled off one of those spike-heeled boots to use like a knife against Kimberley's throat. I held her there against the pulpit where two black candles spat and shivered either side of us. I seized a fistful of blonde hair. The violet rose fascinator pinned to it lacerated my hand while I squealed in pain and fury. That was when I snatched my thick, leather belt from around my father's suit trousers and lashed out. I lashed out once, twice, more...more, until she staggered away from me, away from her beloved Gus and away from the lava-red eyes of Baal.

At that moment, Kimberley lost eye-contact with Baal and he faded fast. His horrific voice, his tantalising eyes, his electric-green misshapen body dulled and dimmed.

I heard my father's voice ring out in the lobby of my mind.

YOU BITCH, KATIE. YOU BITCH!

Out loud, I yelled, "You bastard, Dad. How could you? How could you do this to me?" It was my own voice I heard as I cried out.

Does this mean I've finally won the battle? Am I too strong for you, Kimberley?

I watched, smiling at the back of a black taffeta wedding gown. It rustled violently as Kimberley ran toward the shining arched door, wailing and sobbing, screaming and swearing.

I detest the sound of rustling petticoats.

'I'll be back for you, Guiseppe. One of these days, I'll be back.'

***

I woke in the morning, on top of my bedclothes, streaked with blood and with a brutal headache.

Was it a dream? Or have I clawed at myself during a violent nightmare?

But then, I saw that I clutched a violet silk rose that dripped blood from its pin. One of my spike-heeled boots was missing and I was still dressed in my father's tweed suit.

I laughed inwardly as I bent to remove the itchy suit trousers, relieved that I had won the battle. Against Kimberley. Against my father. Against the demon, Baal.

More fool them. I'm stronger than all of them.

Until a voice whispered from a corner of my bedroom, KA---T----IE...

I might have won the BATTLE. I sure as hell hadn't won the WAR.

'Bring it on!'

And I raised my middle finger to my fornicating father and his wayward bride.

MIGHTY RED

Mighty Red

There's a little red spider mite she comes across, in a dream, when she's eleven years old. As it happens, he's not a figment of her imagination - he's real. He's there when she wakes, lounging happily under the nail of her left big toe. Eagerly awaiting imminent danger. Padding his eight furry, feathery wee legs deep into the dermis of "Left Digit Number One". Staring at her through two tiny black-as-dead-of-night eyes. Ready, set - to go. To squirt spray– yellow or red mist, depending on the task in hand - from his centre. Against any evildoers. Biding his time. Waiting for a catastrophe to happen. His boss, the "Minister of High and Almighty" had warned him that in the days, or years to come, when disasters arise (which they undoubtedly will), it's up to that little red, common-or-garden pest to step up to the plate. For Jasmine. Only her.

Jasmine names him Mighty Red. He calls her Miss Jazz. They quickly form a bond that they believe will never be broken. Not by anybody, or anything. They pledge to keep their eternal secret under wraps. You can count Red among Jazz's best friends. She knows he's there to protect and serve.

Only her. She trusts him to take good care of her. Only her.

A couple of years later, he proves his point – only once – but once is plenty good enough for Jazz.

That one and only near-disaster strikes when Jazz has just turned thirteen. She and her pals are having a rare old time, throwing snowballs, laughing and giggling, when a gang of five boys decide to join in. Only they're wrapping snow around stones to chuck at the girls. One pebble-filled snowball is about to hit Jazz when Red tells her to press her "mite-ready" left big toe with her right heel.

'Go,' he whispers. She presses. And Red hurls an ochre-yellow flare of mist at the stone-filled snowball, redirecting it, somehow, to the boy's belly.

'Oof,' he grunts, 'That bloody hurt.'

'Yeah, I bet.' Jazz grins and bends low to high-five the big toe where Red has his hidey-hole under the nail. His lair.

The little guy, Mighty Red, has only one request for Miss Jazz. He insists that from now on, she always wear peep-toe sandals outside the house. Just as well as it turns out.

'But what if my feet get cold?' she says.

Red assures her he has inbuilt radiation to share, if and when she might need it.

***

Three Year Later

Jasmine Rose is so excited. She's sixteen and this is her first real love-letter.

It comes in a message on her socials. Bordered with rose petals. *Oh, so romantic.* It proclaimed in bold lettering:

JAZZ -
YOU AND I - TOGETHER WE
COULD MAKE
A BED OF PERFECT ROSES

It goes on,

Meet me at Jesmond metro station, next to the Dene, Saturday afternoon, 6 o'clock... xxx

'Yesss!' she yells, waving a fist in the air.

'What was that, Jasmine?' her mother shouts up the stairs.

'Nothing, mam,' Jazz calls back from a bedroom adorned with the Sam Fender posters she and her sister, Lily, collect from teenage pop fan magazines. 'Just watching a movie on the telly.'

'Well, keep the noise down, Jasmine Melanie Rose, if you please. A little decorum would serve you well.'

'Huh,' Jazz whispers, just so her "what-will-the-neighbours-think" mother doesn't hear.

With fingers poised at the keyboard, she types her reply.

Course I'll meet you. Want you and I on a bed of roses too... xxx

* * *

She knows what he'd meant. He'd already told her his name was Nicky Rosario-Steele. Already knows her surname is Rose.

So, Rosario, hmm? Two roses buddying up. Two rose-buddy's, hah! Pardon the pun, she thinks. *That's perfect. We're destined to be an item.*

He's nineteen, he'd said online. *That's perfect too.*

Three years between us.

When she'd sent her photograph to his phone, he'd messaged:

You're a real looker – such a babe.

I could fall in love with your amazing face.

We just got to meet one of these days.

Then, when Nicky's photograph had appeared on Jazz's phone, and a dark-haired, smouldering, brown-eyed, fit guy had gazed at her from the screen, she'd exclaimed out loud,

'Oh, wow, he's PERFECT'.

She'd printed a large glossy copy to show to her sister and her mates just how darned PERFECT he is. He'd told her, one time they were in the chat-room, he was experienced in lovemaking –

(Lovemaking! How quaint, thought Jazz)

- but he'd never found his soul mate, not yet. Then, during one of their long chats, he'd said:

I think you may be the one for me, Jasmine. You look like an angel. You talk like an angel. You must BE an angel.

She'd told Nicky she'd fooled around with boys her own age since she was fourteen; first base, second base - then 'all the way'.

She'd confided to him online:

Stupid kids, that's all they were. But you, Nicky, you're nineteen and so sophisticated and mature. I know it would be different with you.

Came the arrival day of the love letter, they'd already spilled their hearts out over the two months of their internet liaison. Jazz is becoming besotted with Nicky. Nicky had already said he was crazy about "his" Jasmine.

***

She dresses in a short blue dress to match her smoky-azure eyes. She puts a red bow in her hair and flicks layered honey-blonde hair over her shoulders. She's wearing blue sparkly open-toed sandals, like Mighty Red had asked – nay, directed – her to.

'Nicky's gonna adore you,' whispers Gemma, Jazz's best friend and confidante, 'You look ace,' she says, as she helps her with the final touches of face make-up.

Jazz's younger sister, Lily, walks in just as Jazz is throwing a tote bag over her shoulder. 'Where you off to?' she exclaims. 'You look bonny for a change.'

No answer.

'Oh, I knew it. I just knew it. You're going to meet up with that Nicky, aren't you? The sleazy bastard on your chats? Tell me you're not.' She shudders like she's in the throes of a seizure.

'I've had a bad feeling about this lad from the minute it started.'

Lily tries to talk her out of it. Again. 'Meeting him would be a soddin' disaster, Jazz,' she says. 'I mean it. Don't go, sis. Please.'

Jazz laughs that tinkling, infectious giggle of hers, and tells Lily to stop being so silly.

Weeks ago, they'd had almost the same conversation.

Jazz had started up a grand love affair, weeks ago, in that awful chat room on the net. Night after night, she'd messaged him, giggling at his replies.

'What's his name?" Lily had asked her one night, when her busy fingers were flying over the keys, messaging some lad from God knows where.

'Nicky," she'd answered, grinning, "Nice name, hmm? Nicy Steele."

'Nice name? Nicky?' Lily had thrown her arms up in the air. 'Nick-nick! Sounds like a thief an' a robber, Jazz. "Steele" the shirt off yer back! Bloody hell!'

'"Steele" my heart away, more like,' she'd answered, the dimple in her right cheek making her look cute, but she sounded ridiculous and teenage-soppy to Lily. 'He's just fantastic, Sis.'

Both Jazz and Lily have got dimples in their cheeks. They look so much alike and yet their natures are so very different. Lily's the younger, quiet, cautious one: Jazz, fourteen months older, the devil-may-care outgoing one.

Lily had said, 'I don't care how fantastic you think he is. The thought of him scares me a bit, Jazz. He's a stranger. Could be anybody. The bloody mad axeman for all we know. Stay away. Promise me you'll stay away? Just ditch him.'

Ever the sensible sister, is Lily. She rarely takes a chance. Granted, she's intuitive, but Jazz often accuses her of being dull as ditchwater. Lily doesn't give a toss what Jazz thinks of her. Just can't bear her big sister being so feisty and full of herself. Jazz has always been a 'chancer'. Always confident and carefree. A bit of a gambler with life. And like their mam says, from time to time, 'Our Jazz is a proper little madam'.

When Lily had nagged and nagged, on and on, Jazz had capitulated. Anything to shut her up.

'OK, Lil; if it means that much to you, I'll drop him, though I dunno what your problem is. He's sweet, sis: he's really, really sweet.'

So, they'd hugged and done that interlocking of fingers thing they'd do when they made a pact. *All finished and done with.* Though they'd known, both of them, in the marrow of their bones, it wasn't done with. Jazz had fibbed. Not intentionally, maybe. But not for the first time, either.

***

'I'm off, Mam,' Jazz shouted from the staircase, hopping and skipping to the front door. 'Me an' Gemma's away to the town. Dunno what time I'll be back, but no later than the last Metro – promise.' She didn't tell her mum where she was going, hadn't ever told her about her chat room romance.

'See you later, Lil. I'll tell you all about it when I get back,' she grinned at Gemma and stuck her tongue out at her little sister. Then she slammed the front door behind her, as Lily answered,

'Yeah, right,' adding, for effect: 'You bloody liar, you.'

***

They set off for Tynemouth Metro station, her and Gemma. Jazz had to travel what she called 'the wrong way round' via the coast to get to Jesmond. She'd be able to look out to sea if she sat on the left side. Watch the little yachts on the white waves of the North Sea. And daydream about Nick.

He'll be waiting when I press the button to get off the train.

Gemma is giving it large about Lily's cheek and sass, all the way to the Metro. Saying she has no respect for her elder sister.

'Aye, well, serves me tight, really, Gem. I tell her lies; she believes me. Tell her the truth; she doesn't believe a word I say. Hah! I can't win.'

'Truth? Like what?' Gemma asks.

'You probably won't believe me, neither.'

''Course I will, Jazz. Unless it's one of your daft stories.'

'Alright, then. What I'm gonna tell you is the absolute truth. Honest. But I bet you any money you think I'm making it up. Lil didn't believe me. Might as well have been a fairy tale, far as she was concerned.'

'Not me, Jazz. 'Fess up, then?'

'OK, then.' They were sat on a bench against the wall of the platform travelling Via the Coast. As they wiggle their ankles and wriggle their toes, Jazz points to her unsheathed, sandalled left big toe.

She said, 'Ever noticed that before?'

'Yeah, 'course. Your tattoo.'

'It's not a tattoo, Gem. It's a little red spider mite. Been there since I was eleven. Give his furry little legs a stroke. But not hard. Be gentle.'

So Gemma does. And squeals. 'Ugh. It's like it moved,' she says. 'You've got a hairy toe. You should shave it.'

'I told you, it's a real live spider mite, Gem. Lives there under the nail. Got me out of a scrape, once. Says he will again, when I need him.'

'Yeah, right! "Across the Spider-Verse". It's a tattoo, ya daft bat.'

Jazz stares, glares – and runs toward the approaching train, pushing her way into the carriage to sit on the left for the view, her back arched toward an astonished Gemma.

'Bitch,' murmurs Jazz. Under her breath. Fighting the tears. Thinks she might never tell the truth to anyone again, ever.

***

She glances at her watch as she sprints her way up the steps, past the bright red, blue and yellow geometric design on the wall. And out of Jesmond metro station.

Ten past six. I'm late. Bloody trains. Always late.

Her eyes glistened tears as she darted a look past the tall white statues.

Not here. Not coming...or he's gone.

'Hello, Jasmine,' says a husky male voice. 'Pleased to meet you. I'm Nick's dad, Jason." He smiled a crooked, dentured smile and held out a nicotine-stained hand.

"Where's Nicky?" Feigning nonchalance, she adjusted the denim jacket over her sky blue dress rather than shake hands with this wrinkly old man in front of her.

Must be at least forty. Not bad-looking in a James Bond older-guy sorta way! Doesn't look a bit like Nick though.

'It's OK, darlin', he sent me to meet you. Unavoidable delayed, he said. Come on, girl, he'll likely be home by now. By the way, nice long legs.'

Ignoring the comment, Jazz's sensitive turned-up nose smells lemon and patchouli.

Mmmm … nice.

'Does Nicky vape, too?" she asks, panting, striving to keep up with Jason in her blue three-inch open-toed stilettos.

Jason exclaims, 'Smell it, can you? Disappointed in Nick's dad, are you, Jasmine, sweetheart?'

Jazz says something like, no, not at all, she really likes some of the vape scents.

'How far we going?' They'd turned left out of the station and crossed at the traffic lights.

'Next on the right. There in a couple of mo's,' Jason replies, looking her up and down with interest.

'Don't like me much, do you?' Jazz blurts out, 'You're looking down your nose at me, I reckon'.

"Oh, not a bit of it. I like you well enough, Jasmine." A wide grin displays plump, pouty, almost feminine lips and pink, high cheek-bones.

Not bad for an old guy, Jazz thinks. Still, a shivery tingle runs down her spine, making her a little nervous. She scrapes around in her handbag, feeling for the dog-eared edge of Nicky's photograph – the one she'd showed off to her sister and mates. For reassurance.

Jason takes a key from his pocket and heads up the path of a house with a tiny walled garden, overgrown with a mixture of yellow roses, lavender and … nettles? *Bit of a dump, Jazz, underneath the showy stuff.*

'Here we are, Jasmine, my sweet. Time for your love-in with Nicky, is it?'

Love-in! What the hell's a love-in? Does he wanna spy on us? Watch me in my underwear?

'Nicky, she's here," Jason hollers up the hall stairs as he pushes Jazz through the open door. "In you go, Little Summer Jasmine..."

'Don't *call* me that. You don't know me well enough to give me pet names.'

Jazz has suddenly had enough. There's something sadly wrong here. She feels it coursing through her. Her left big toe is throbbing. Vibes from Mighty Red. He's on Red Alert, she's sure. Getting ready for war.

Twisting her face in annoyance, she yells, 'I'm not stayin' if *you're* gonna be hangin' around, old man.'

Her voice shakes as she calls out, lifting her chin to the landing 'I'm goin' home, Nicky. Your dad's doing my head in. Send me a text.' Her words echo in the damp narrow hallway.

'AND WHERE THE HELL ARE YOU?'

As Jazz spins around toward the front door, Jason forces her shoulders hard against the flocked wallpaper.

'Oh, no you don't, little girl. You're here an' you're staying, long as I want you.' He laughs as he dead-bolts the lock. Puts the key in his trouser pocket.

'What do you think you're doin'?'

'You not catchin' on, little Jasmine Rose!' He grabs her bag from her tight grip, upturns it, takes out her phone and smashes it with the heel of his booted foot.

He chuckles, 'There *is* no Nicky Rosario-Steele'. *I›m* your chat room lover. ME! Gotcha good n' proper, eh? Go figure, Little Summer Jasmine.'

'What...? But what about the photo?' She stares at Nicky's image smiling up at her from the Maplewood flooring where it had fallen from her tote bag.

'Don't be daft. You're not half naïve, silly girl. Got the photo from the net. Model, I think. Or a rent boy, hah! I've left no traces, case you think somebody'll come lookin'. Welcome to your new life,' he gloats, lighting a cigarette from a crumpled pack, blowing smoke-rings onto her tear-stained face.

Jazz bends down, snatches up the photograph and tears it to shreds. 'You bastard. My mum, my sister – they'll come find me.'

'Keep on wishing, girl. But for now, let's get you into some decent clothes. You look like a tart.'

Jason slaps her hard across her flushed cheeks, tears the red bow from her ringleted caramel-and-gold hair and leers a hateful smile that attempts to loosen Jazz's bladder. But the brave girl hangs on to her dignity.

As he pushes a pile of dowdy, servile garments into her arms, he pulls her trembling body toward him, grips her dimpled chin and hisses:

'Now get changed, slave, an' wipe off that disgusting make-up. Ain't gonna be the bed of roses you dreamed about, stupid cow.' With that, Jason (or whoever he is) turns, laughs, leaves the room and locks the door from the outside.

Mighty Red consoles Miss Jazz, whispering instructions that only she can hear. How she manages to interpret those tiny squeaks, she'll never know. But she does. She bursts into tears. Grateful. Anticipating a solution. If it'll work.

'Of course it will,' squeals a full-of-excitement Mighty Red.

**

If it seems to Lily that it's well past the arrival of the last metro, she's not wrong.

She's just surfaced from a troubled sleep – and it must be way past midnight.

Jazz's bed is empty. Lily's duvet is in a messed-up, sweaty heap. She doesn't like the sinking feeling she's getting, waking up next to her big sister's empty bed, looking neat, pristine and unslept in.

Jazz had promised their mother – PROMISED – she'd be home before – or on - the last Metro. She'd told fibs again. Perjured herself - AGAIN.

You're a liar, Jazz. I could kill you for this!

She's really got the collywobbles now – the bloody heebie-jeebies - and she doesn't know what to do.

Text her. That's what I'll do

WHERE R U?

She sends it and waits for an answer, twisting her dark-blonde hair into curls. The tresses slide away from her hand as she twists. She's not sure if it's natural sheen or it's sweat. Because Lily's sweating like a bull.

Minutes go by and no answer. She's expecting a DON'T WORRY BE HAPPY? message - but nothing happens. The minutes turn into five, ten. fifteen.

She glances at the Minnie Mouse alarm clock on the bedside table. One o'clock in the morning.

'This isn't good,' she says aloud. Past herself now, she's starting to feel sick.

My sister's in trouble – I can feel it coming from wherever the hell she is. My stomach's making acid-flavoured yoghurt.

Gasping, bent double, Lily retches and falls to her knees.

'Oh, Jazz: what have you done?' Lily yells what she expects will probably be a blood-curdling scream but it comes out like "Eeek". Hiccups jump out of her lungs in a spine-tingling frenzy of fear for her sister. And she's angry – so angry.

Speed-dialling her number, she waits, drumming fingers on the Bambi rug between the beds – but it's gone straight to voice-mail. She looks around frantically. All this kids' stuff in the room –

'What the ffff... Grow up Lil,' She's screeching from the centre of her heart, thinking aloud, *'What now? Oh, God, what now?',*

Lily tosses her sparkly, pink iPhone onto Jazz's empty bed. 'Frozen' illustrations of Elsa, Anna and Olaf gaze at her from its glittery cover. *Kids' stuff.*

The girls were given phones for their last birthdays, 'to keep you both safe,' Mam had said. So why doesn't Jazz answer? Tell Lil she's safe?

Glaring into the dressing table mirror, the one that they fight over to do their make-up, she sees a ghostly reflection of a pale, pasty face that should look tanned and healthy. A reflection of how she looks right now. Worried and terrified.

And Lily runs. Out of the creaky bedroom door and down the hall to where their mother is sleeping, ready to shout,

'It's our Jazz! Mam! She's in trouble. I just know it.'

But she doesn't. The floodgates are opening. Instead, Lily cries a waterfall of tears that soak into the landing carpet, as she waits and waits, sobs and sobs.

Weeps herself into a heap of sleep – until she's wakened with a thump in the rump.

***

A bare left foot hovers in front of Lily's half-shut eyes.

'Whaaaa …' she croaks. 'Oh, Jazz, you're back.' She throws herself around her sister's neck like a hangman's noose. Grabs Jazz's wrists. Feels for a pulse.

'Yep. Looks like I'm definitely in the land of the living,' says Jazz, 'Thanks to Mighty Red here. My little furry-legged friend. Eh, boy?'

'Who?' says Lily.

'Never mind. You wouldn't believe me, anyway.'

'What about this Nicky, then?'

'There is no Nicky. Doesn't exist.'

'Eh?'

'Yep. No Nick. Just a pervy predator posing as his dad.'

'No!'

'Yes, Lily. Truth, whole truth. Nothing but the truth.'

'Tell me?'

'OK then. Come downstairs. Be quiet. And listen. No lies – promise.'

Jazz talked Lily through the whole ordeal. About the bloke who said he was Nicky's dad and walked her to a terraced house in Jesmond.

'There was just something about him that made me wary. We got scared didn't we, Red?'

'Go on. This is getting weird. Your foot's twitching, do you know?'

''Course I know. Mighty Red's shaking like a leaf. Aren't you, boy?' Jazz wiggles her left big toe. 'He saved my life. And if you don't wanna believe me, I'll shut up right now. Then all you need to know is, we got away. Eventually. Up to you, Lil. But this is a true account, word for word. OK? Give a squeak, little mite? For Lily?'

And he does. Red squeaks. Not as loudly as a dog toy – but loud enough for Lily to hear.

'Sold! Highest bidder!' she says. 'He squeaked like a mouse. Who'd have thought it.'

'Don't interrupt me then.' Jazz, in command mode, says, 'Not a word.'

***

Jazz relives what happened, holding Lily's hand all the while. When she reaches the point where she's locked into a room that holds nothing but a double bed and a pair of blackout curtains, she begins to cry. And between sobs, sighs and snuffles, she tells the story of the deadly near-miss of their dreadful ordeal.

'The knock on the door came as a shock. We'd waited in that locked, poky, badly lit room for what seemed like hours. Red had told me not to remove my clothes, not to wear the crappy, dowdy outfit this "Jason" person had told me to change into. I knew exactly what to do when "Jason" came charging in like a madman. Only he didn't – charge in, that is. He knocked.

So, I said 'Yes, Jason. Ready,' hoping I sounded compliant enough.

In he came, smirking like some nasty old gremlin, or ogre, or whatever. His face dropped when he saw I was still in my blue dress – what he thought of as my 'tart's outfit'. I heard Red's squeak - 'DO IT NOW' - and I bent forward, pressing my left big toe where Red has his hidey-hole. I pressed as hard as I could on that little red body.

It was as if I'd said, 'Hey Presto' or 'Abracadabra' or whatever. A thick spray of red stuff came streaming out of my little friend's belly, into the Perv's left eye, then his right eye. It was brilliant. Woo-hoo! Nasty piece of shit screamed like a Banshee, cried like a big, overgrown baby, holding on to his eyelids like he'd been blinded by lightning – or hellfire. Super-amazing!

'I can't see. Everything's gone black.' Screaming the place down, he was, in a Sunderland accent. Proper Mackem. 'Help me. Help me!' He's trying to reach me in the dark – or the blackness - or something. Holding his arms out in front of him like he's playing "Blind Man's Buff" at a kids' Christmas party.

That's when Red said, 'Let's get out of here. Now.'

I said, 'Gimme the keys out your pocket, you old perv.' Threw my blue stiletto heels at him; caught him on his chin. He reeled backward.

He didn't give me the keys. I reckon he was a bit preoccupied, so I just took them. Grabbed my bag, unlocked the deadbolts and turned the key. We were out, legging it up the road, hell for leather, me whooping-and-hollering, little Red squeaking like he'd won an Olympic Gold.

We did stop on the way home - that nine-mile, tedious, penniless, without-a-bank-card walk. What else could we do? Couldn't just leave it there.

So, I knock on the end door – number 2 – loud with voices on a TV movie. I'm holding a Bic-penned note I'd scribbled onto a scrap of lined notebook paper. Found it in my tote-bag. It's my story; my abridged story - excluding any reference to Mighty Red. Nobody would take that seriously. Nobody would accept there'd be thanks to give to Red and his "Minister of High and Almighty" for his heaven-sent help.

I'm clutching the key to number 42, the House of Horrors, in a tight grip. I'm holding on to my scrawled list of events, sans anything "Mighty Red".

When a tiny, twinkle-eyed old lady answers the door, I ask her to call the police, pass on the door key, give the cops my note of explanation – my story.

Will she do that? I ask. I'm scared to put my name out there – to the police, or anyone. I don't want to sell my story to the papers. I just want this guy at number 42 stopped.

'Good for you,' says the sweet old lady in a Geordie, "butter wouldn't melt" kindly tone. 'Bloody nonce bastard's been at it for years. Never, ever got done for it. No proof, see. Mebbes you've got proof? I'd like to bloody think so. Paedophile, that's what 'e is, pet. Wanna come in for a cup o' tea? Bonny lass like you shouldn't be standin' there on a freezin' caad night.'

'No thanks, missus,' say I, 'Gotta get off home. It's a bit of a hike. Lovely to meet you.'

There's silence in the room. Stunned magic in the air. Except for a couple of little squeaks from someone's left big toe –

"Praise to the High and Almighty!"

À
La Carte
Alley

À La Carte Alley

D usk's mauve mantle dips its corners into oily puddles, until a dark veil envelops daylight's flush into the blackness of night. It's November, and cold as Jack Frost's fingers.

In this wasteland of overflowing rusty bins, a mangle-eared ginger tom-cat casts an eye to the sushi-bar's high wall that sits between the strip joint and the greasy spoon cafe. Cutting a dashing figure in the shadows of the grimy alley in London's sleazy Soho, making a jaunty jump to the wall's weed-ridden top, he licks a muddy ginger paw.

Pete, the pimple-faced kitchen hand, grunts, "Gerr-away, yer flea-filled moggie," as he rolls a cigarette with skinny tobacco-stained fingers and lights it with a flourish.

'You comin' out, Gus? I'll be outside the door in the back lane. Yer know what the owner's like. An' the bloody government. No smokin' on the premises. Not even a sneaky one.'

'Yeah. Mamma-Mia. Crazy ain't it?' Guiseppe shouts from inside the restaurant kitchen, a hint of Italian blending with his gruff East–End London accent.

'Still raining, is it? Bloody rain. England, huh? Rain, rain, rain.'

Murky drizzle descends into the moonless night onto a bedraggled silver-grey kitten clawing at a laid-open supermarket sack, rooting around for treasure. His rump wriggles in a burning desire to find an edible bit of chow in these Badlands of left-over food.

'Hey, Gus, come an' check out this little kitty-cat. Can't be more than a couple months old. He's a sight cuter than those chewed-up-lookin' dog-eared ol' moggy cats you usually feed.'

'Been comin' around for a few weeks on an' off, that one' Guiseppe says from behind Pete.

'An' call me Chef, will ya?' He combs his high, greasy quiff of hair with his fingers.

His tall, white hat flickers ghostly and cloud-like, as the moon chooses to show a wedge of its eerie, glow-in-the-dark face. Thread-bare, blue-chequered trousers, stretched taut around plump thighs, hang limp and loose around white-socked ankles – part of his trademark "Teddy-Boy of the fifties" look. He's certainly old enough to carry it off. Proper old-timer.

'Christ, I nearly jumped out me skin. Give it up, will yer, sneakin' up on me. Yes Chef, no Chef, three bags full, Chef. Happy now?" he chuckles, showing off the dimple in his chin.

'You are but a bloody insolent bambino, Pete.'

'Yeah, right. Anyway, look at this little feller. What d'you think? Little corker, isn't he?'

Head popping out beneath rusty cans and slime-festooned bottles, the kitten spits out a deep green cabbage leaf, much to Guiseppe and young Pete's delight. They watch him sniffing with high expectation at a meaty morsel in his tiny, clawed grasp.

Chef opens a plastic bag, containing a handful of à la carte appetizers he brings into the alley every night. Chucks a couple of tender meatballs the grey kitten's way, meatballs as big as the kitten's head.

'Here you go. Hi-O Silver, away!'

Another Nifty-Fifties homage. Lone Ranger, wasn't it? That TV show my nan watched, Pete thinks.

With a sharp "meow", the silver-furred kitten runs toward the brick wall surrounding the restaurant.

'That small-fry little guy is game, isn't he? Confident little feral lad, he is. You can tell he's a survivor. Watch him go.' Chef points to the kitten ascending the grey-bricked wall with the lightning speed of a rocket.

As the kitten joins Ginger Tom to show off his new-found Italian meatballs, Guiseppe smiles, 'First time I seen them two sit together. Ginger can get a bit possessive o' that wall. He must be getting soft, or somethin'. Or maybe Silver's getting well-hard.'

Then Ginger hisses, mewling open-mouthed disgust at Kittie's boldness. Jerking a tattered, scarred tail, he sends a haughty message in Silver's direction.

Beat a retreat, he seems to be saying.

"Yer spoke too soon, mate. Ginger's the boss cat, far as I can see," Pete remarks, blowing smoke rings upward into the murky, foggy night.

'Go on, Kittie. You stand yer ground,' Pete hollers, nudging Guiseppe and stamping on his cigarette butt. 'He doesn't give a monkey's,' he adds, watching Silver's back arch, spikes of fuzzy, grey-white fur standing upright in comic relief. Sputtering a pink-tongued mewl at Ginger, little Silver makes it clear he's staying put.

'Need to get back in an' clear up, Pete. You get goin' an' I'll just finish me smoke. Save these cats proper nice plates o' goodies, will yer, son? They need a good dinner on a nasty night like this. Cold weather eats into yer bones.'

"They're cats, for cryin' out loud. Got fur coats. Yer crackers, you are, Gus. You've already got a bag o' treats in yer arms for them.'

'They're just kitty entrées, cheeky young man.'

The kitchen hand grins as he saunters back into the warmth of the kitchen, 'Daft as a brush you are. Ain't you … Chef?'

Guiseppe ignores the boy. 'An' double check the customers 'ave all gone, will yer? Don't want nobody locked in.'

'Yeah, I will, Chef. You comin' next door to the boozer when we done? Promised us a lock-in'

''s'ppose so. Sid and Johnny goin' too?'

'Think they've already shot the coop.'

***

Guiseppe leans forward, hands on chunky knees to get a better look at something he saw moving on the ground.

'There you are, yer little sod,' he whispers to a gleaming, yellow-eyed rat with sharp white teeth emerging from between two torn and soggy cardboard boxes. "Ugly little blighter. Cats'll have yer if yer don't watch out.'

He peers at the rat, watching its eyes narrow, its whiskers quivering in the breeze as it places a lean paw into the gloom. Picking out a glob of pale, yellow gunk sitting atop a greying mush of cauliflower, it nibbles with discernment.

'It's as well you're not fussy, like me cat-pals, eh? You'll eat anything, you mangy rat.'

Guiseppe stamps a foot to scare the rat away. He scrunches his eyes in an attempt to make out the rat's shape in the miserable grey hues of the night. He's lost sight of it – but Ginger's on it in a flash, hindquarters rippling in an abstract maze of blush-red shades.

Little Silver watches Ginger too. Diminutive ears cocked, tail swishing back and forth, he observes the action – acting the apprentice to the master. But the rat has got clean away.

"Never mind, you two. There're plenty more tasty bits for you inside. I'll go get 'em, will I? Wait there."

Guiseppe clicks his tongue twice, taking off his chef's hat to smooth his startling black quiff of hair. As he flicks his cigarette in a glowing cascade of crimson embers and strolls back to the sushi-bar's kitchen, he's thinking,

Reckon the staff all know I dye my hair. Grecian 2000 or something. Mamma Mia, my wife sure looks after me good.

Thinking about his wife, Gus gets caught in a reverie about their lack of children. Just as well Maria didn't particularly consider that having a family was necessary to their marriage. She was only thirty-two when heavy periods and fibroids lead to her needing a hysterectomy. Maria, always the sensible one – and the romantic one, actually – said they didn't need children; they had each other.

'What about pets?' Guiseppe had asked Maria, a few years later.

'Mio caro marito' she'd said, 'I'm allergic to all things furry.'

And that was that. No kids; no pets. Yet he found himself attracted to being some sort of dad; drawn more and more to the idea, as the years dragged on. Hence his love of these feral beauties hanging around the back of the restaurant. Known as "À La Carte Alley", it was his favourite place to be. These strays and ferals became his heart's desire, his large, furry family.

***

'Grub's up, kitties!' Guiseppe's pock-marked red face leaks sweat, dripping down onto a wobbling double chin.

The latch clicks. Two alley cats turn. Their preternatural green eyes scrutinise the silhouette that opens the creaking slatted alley door. Guiseppe has changed into what he calls his "civvies". He runs his hands down his best black drape jacket and clicks the heels of the crepe soled shoes he's wearing: the ones he likes to call his "creepers".

'Where's all yer mates, eh, lads?' Gus wants to know. 'Bring them over to Daddy.'

Soon as he says that word, "Daddy", they all come running down the alley for their nightly banquet. At least twenty cats run and jump toward him. Black ones, white ones, tabby, ginger and smoky ones - golden-eyed, green-eyed, blue-eyed, you name it.

Tails up, eyes glittering with expectations of full bellies, they wrap their bodies around Chef, purring, weaving around the ankles of the man whose plump arms are laden with plastic platters of fish and carboard dishes of meat. Guiseppe carries the plates, waiter-style, on his hands and up to the crooks of his elbows.

'Gonna be friends, all you kitties, while you get yer dinner? No fightin' you hear?'

Chef smiles down on his feline friends, stroking damp matted fur coats with huge rough hands. They reply with mewls and slinky greetings.

***

'You gonna talk to those bloody moggies all night, Gus? It's all finished in here. Benches are gleamin', pots are washed. You comin'?' Pete yells from behind the open kitchen door.

'Not be long, son," Guiseppe continues to pat the cats around their ears as he glances sideways at Pete's skinny frame. "Just need to get these fellas sorted out, don't we, Kitties, eh? Don't we now? Poor devils are starvin'.'

'Starvin'? That'll be the day. You treat them cats like bloody kings. Feed the bloody cat neighbourhood, yer do.'

'An' who wouldn't eh? They're my little family, after all.' A tear rolls down Chef's cheek.

Uh – oh. Thinking about my Maria and all her troubles has opened the floodgates. Hope Pete didn't notice. They'll laugh their socks off at me all night for being so soft..

'Yer losin' yer marbles, Chef, yer are. Family! Wait till I tell the lads about Chef's cat family.'

'An' what if yer do, eh? Who gives a bugger? Not me.' He changes tack quickly, feeling defensive. 'Tell you what, Pete? Lock the front door behind you an' shove the keys in the letter box. I'll lock up from the back door. I'm all done once I get these plates in an' washed up.'

'Right you are, Chef. See you in the club. I'll have a pint o' Guiness waiting for yer.'

'Molte Grazie, Pete. Don't tell the wife about the after-hours lock-in at the club.'

'She'd have a bloody hissy-fit – I know.'

'Yep – bloody hissy-fit's right. Maybe even a heart attack. Gi's ten minutes an' I'll be with yer. An' leave it out about what I just said.'

'Yes ... Chef.' Pete winks. 'Ah, well, *family* first. Cats, eh?'

'Cheeky blighter. Ciao for now. Wish this bloody rain would stop.'

***

It seems that no time at all has past since Pete left the restaurant that all four of Guiseppe's limbs begin to shake. His mouth opens in a violent intake of breath. He gasps. He jerks upright. Stiffens like a guard on parade.

He's thinking, *It's an omen. Should never have said those words, "heart attack". Stupid bloody Guiseppe. Balardo! I summoned Malocchio, the Evil Eye.*

He's been sitting on an upturned oil-drum watching. Watching his moggy family chewing, spitting, swallowing. Purring keenly at their glorious à la carte nosh.

"Pete...Pete," he mouths, but no sound comes out.

Gus looks comical as he rises to a halt. Stock-still, like a soldier saluting his commander. The cats look up at their friend and mentor with interest. They watch his eyes blink in rapid motion, again and again, until they glaze over. They back off a little as their dear Guiseppe clutches the front of his white shirt, fingers kneading the black shoe-string tie knotted around his tightening collar. They stare at his sweaty cheeks shining in the foggy dim light of a partially clouded silver-grey moon. The shrieking of cat calls seems to almost collide with Chef's colour. A kaleidoscope of stark blues and purples gleam on his bloated, rigid face.

Seconds pass as Guiseppe teeters back and forth on rubber soles. His thick-calved legs judder in his drainpipe jeans. His trouser bottoms stick to his calves with streams of perspiration. His arms shoot down to his sides, taut and wooden as a marionette's. He begins to topple toward the trash cans and the slick, wet ground.

Cats in all shapes and sizes race behind their adoptive 'daddy', catching his shoulders with their paws and claws, lowering him gently to the cobbled lane.

Piles of rubbish scatter and slosh into dirty rain-filled potholes. Kittens howl high-pitched squeals and dance in a frenzy, away from the metallic clatter of bin-lids. Ginger has already sought a place on the high grey wall. He's gazing down at the mayhem, paws pointing, like he's conducting an orchestra.

In the dim haze of swirling mist, the glowing amethyst hue of Guiseppe's skin turns a vivid bruised-purple, shades of indigo spreading like ghostly fingers, dulling to a mottled blue-black. The cats move nearer to their portly friend, inquisitive paws reaching out to touch him. The death-rattle that gurgles in Guiseppe's throat builds to a deadly crescendo until all is silent.

Silent but for the purring kitten breathing into the blue-tinged mouth of a dead man. Silent, bar the rhythm of many a cat's paws padding - up and down, up and down - into Guiseppe's huge chest. Silent, save the high-pitched squeak from the golden rat as he glides with stealth toward the mountain of flesh looming before him. Silent, except for the low growls in multiple cats' throats, warning the rat away from their fast-cooling friend.

* * *

Though only five minutes or so have gone by, Pete, Johnny and Sid come looking for Chef. Pete had said he had a "bad feeling". Didn't know why.

'Let's pop back, then. Can't do no 'arm,' Sid had said, glugging the rest of his pint.

'You two go. Can't be arsed,' said Johnny.

'Lazy sod. Come on, I'll set up the next round afore we go.'

'Don't like the look of this," Sid peers through the glass window of the restaurant's kitchen, seeing nothing except the glow of a bunch of keys in the darkness. "Let's check round back.'

"Get an ambulance, Sid," Pete yells, racing through the puddles in the alley to where the chef lies prone on the debris-littered ground.

"Get those bloody animals off 'im," Johnny shouts, fit to burst Pete's eardrum.

Several cats slink away from Guiseppe's body, hissing and spitting as Sid shoos them away from his boss. But the moggies move no more than a few yards, hunkering down - watching. Some don't shift at all. They're getting on with the task in hand.

'We're too late, Sid. No pulse – nothin'," Pete announces. 'He's a goner. An' there's too many cats to count. So many bloody cats. Tell you what I think. I think they're doing CPR. Mouth-to-mouth. Or standing guard. Trying to take care of 'im.'

'Don't be bloody daft, Pete.' Sid and Johnny can't help but laugh at Pete's outburst.

Looking down at the motionless body on the damp concrete slabs, Pete whispers, 'Don't you worry, Gus, mate, I'll feed yer little pals now you've gone. Just like you'd want me to.'

At that, the big ginger tom called Ginger, jumps onto Gus's chest and thumps him with a hefty paw; BANG - right on the Chef's sternum.

There's a noisy intake of breath, a throaty "aaarrrggghh" and Guiseppe opens his eyes. Sea-bright irises gleam with tears. Bushy eyebrows change shape into a question-mark.

'Whaaaa…' he groans as he sits up, staring into space. Then he smiles.

'See that, fellers? They saved me. You saved me, you little rascals. Keyholders of my life, you are. My feline family – an' you Pete, say nothin' figlio; you young reprobate.'

When the paramedics arrive to haul Gus off to hospital for treatment and a check-over, one of them scratches his head and says:

'Cats doin' first aid? Never heard anything like it in my life.'

Another one says, 'Well, well. well. Seems the new meaning of CPR is – "Cat Paw Resuscitation".

THE DISSOCIA-TIVE ASSOCIATE

The
Dissociative Associate

2045 - Prologue

It took until this year, 2045 - our 95th birthdays - for the shit to hit the fan. How did this "Very-Hellish-Event" happen to us twenty-four years ago, or indeed, where did its name come from? Oh, we're about to tell you. All in good time. As to "why", we can only guess. Suffice to say, it *did* happen. This "Event" changed our lives for all time.

We three became four, out of sheer necessity. Three, securely protected by the fourth; our associate and cling-film wraparound.

In 2021, climate change was affecting the planet in calamitous ways. Oceans ogled the land, seas snaffled the coastlines, rivers rose, waters deepened. What better way to move forward, than to forever cruise the canals with Helvetica, our helmsperson of the waters. I mean, who knows how long we might live?

2045 – The Accident

'You're awake. Welcome back to the world.'

'What? Where in hell am I?'

'Certainly not Hell. Hexham Hospital. Dr Frank at your service.' The doctor pushed his fingers through rich, reddish-blond hair.

'Just a few details. You came to us without ID.'

His patient gave a glittery, blue-eyed stare, pushing thick blonde hair behind her ear.

'So,' ignoring her gaze, he said, 'Jane Doe? Your real name would help.'

The patient answered with amusement, spoken in posh-northern.

'Sure thing. I'm Helvetica Reising-Uppard.'

'Unusual name.'

'Well, that's what my passport says. What happened? How did I get here?'

'You were run over by a car, thrown in the air and landed, believe it or not, clutching a hedgehog. Not a mark on you or the critter. The driver had to be treated for shock. *You've* been unconscious for two days.'

'And how's the little feller. Is he OK?'

'I told you. In shock…'

'Not the *driver*; the hedgehog. He was terrified. Curled up into the tiniest ball. Call me Elvish. It's my nickname.

'Elvis? You a fan?'

'Not Elvis. I said *Elvish*. Face like a pixie's. See?' She cupped her face to prove it. 'He OK? We love animals.'

Dr Frank paused for a moment. 'So, who's *we*, Elvish?'

'My friends and I.' She pointed to the left side of her head.

'The hedgehog's fine. In a sanctuary nearby. May I be frank with you?'

'I suppose. You *are* Frank, after all.' She giggled, blushed a little.

'The thing is, while you were - erm, sleeping – you spoke in three very different voices. Different tones, different accents – not at all like your own.'

'Yeah. Took one hell of a lot of elocution lessons to get it right.'

'Sorry, I don't quite ...'

Helvetica cut in abruptly, waving aside his words with fluttery palms, 'The voices would be my friends, my 'little-old-ladies'. I'm their agent and publisher. We're very close, you understand. And I sleep-talk. Loudly. Always have.'

'You pointed – here,' indicating his temple, 'That's quite telling in psychology. Is it possible, Helvetica, that these three voices live in your head?'

'Don't believe everything you hear, Doc. But hey, they're all real. Alive and well. Writing books, pamphlets, articles in journals. You can check. Verity Ingleby, Helen Rice, Patricia Appleyard. All aged 95. All born October 1950. Still kicking around. And booting me up the backside at every opportunity.'

Helvetica gave Dr Frank her best "Elvish" smile.

Dr Frank jotted a few words in a notebook. 'Can we meet in my office for a chat later, Elvish.' He put out a hand, squeezed her palm. 'All very interesting. Just one or two things I need to verify.'

'You think I'm crazy, don't you?'

'Not at all. I do think you may have what some people call "split personality" or in medical terms, "dissociative identity disorder". We'll get to the bottom of it.'

Helvetica's eyes widened, paled to a lighter blue, eyelids changing shape and deepening. Even her face became more rounded and full-cheeked.

'It all stems from the weirdest weekend in Lake Windermere, 2021.' She said it – not intentionally - in a bold Liverpool accent, '*They* call it "The Event"'.

She blushed. Hoped he hadn't noticed the change in accent. What if he had? *Oh God*, she thought, *that would be cat out of the bag. Stay hidden, Helen.*

Dr Frank seemed puzzled. Leaving the room, he murmured, 'Intriguing.'

***

After a nurse had settled her, Helvetica (call me Elvish), waved her away and wandered into the bathroom to freshen up.

While peering at her blurred image in the mirror, it's *they* who gazed back. A haze shimmered around the edges of the reflection. Shadowy females glimmered, in flickering motion. The reflection, looking wrinkled and old at first, then appearing youthful. The impression was of a twenty-something, constantly blonde but shifting in facial appearance. It was as though she stood in a hall of mirrors at the funfair – wiggly, wavy-lined and weird.

She shook herself to get rid of how overwhelmed she felt. Mumbling to herself, Helvetica tapped her temple. 'I can't do this. Can't shut you three out. Dr Frank will cotton on - and I'll end up in the loony bin.'

'No, you won't. Git yersel' sorted, lass.' What came out of her mouth was high-pitched in a West Cumbrian dialect. Looking back toward the mirror, she noticed her forehead heighten, her lips thicken.

'Dammit, Verity, stay hidden. I want to crawl into a dark hole and sleep. Forever.'

'Is someone in there with you?' The ward clerk knocked, shouting through the bathroom door. 'It's just that Dr Frank is waiting.'

'Coming.' Helvetica cringed.

***

'Come on in. Relax for a bit.'

'Thanks, Doc, but I'm still a bit woolly-headed. I'd rather do this tomorrow, if ...'

'Won't keep you long. Bear with me.'

She perched on the proffered, comfy-looking couch.

'But, first, tell me a little bit about yourself.'

'Thought I had. Publisher, agent ...'

'Not that. Where is it you live, exactly?'

'Mostly on my narrowboat, up and down the canals. Sometimes here in Hexham at Tricia's place. Sometimes over in West Cumbria with Verity. Sometimes New Brighton at Helen's.'

'Nomads, eh? Interesting. So how long have you been hanging around with these three ladies?'

'Ladies? Why, no, man. Certainly not ladies.' A loud guffaw erupted from Helvetica's throat, the accent, well-to-do Geordie. Her nostrils flared; a dimple appeared in her chin. Her eyes glowed a stunning aquamarine.

Dr Frank stared in bewilderment. Wrote something down in his notebook. Lifted an index finger. Smirked through a well-whiskered chin.

'You realise, you've spoken in three entirely different accents, Elvish?'

Not waiting for an answer, he went on, 'I've looked up your friends. Sight nor sound of them since 2021 apart from books and articles. Ones that *you've* published, Helvetica. Your colleagues are Doctors in Psychology, Psychiatry. Philosophy, right?' I've checked photographs of all of you. Not one picture of your friends after 2021 – though lots before then. Pictures of you only start appearing after your friends *disappear* off the face of the earth.

The doctor took off a pair of rimless spectacles, pointing them toward her, 'Are these friends alive or dead? Or do they exist in your imagination? I'd appreciate an honest answer.'

Helvetica's cheeks turned asbestos white. 'They're real. Of course they're real. I'm with them all the time. Their associate, general dogsbody, spare part …'

Her words trailed off as she stood up, jelly-legged, pointing at Doctor Frank.

'You! Soft lad. Leave her be. Leave her alone.' The Scouser accent pronounced "her" as "hair".

Crashing to the floor, her NHS dressing gown tangled up around her, Helvetica yelled,

'You'll upset the applecart, Helen. You and your big Scouse mouth.'

Dr Frank rushed toward Helvetica. Checked her vitals. Seemed contemplative, fist on chin, 'That you in there, Helen? Helen Rice? Doctor of Psychology? Talk to me.'

And Helen did. But not before Dr Frank asked the question, 'Who was it coined the name, "Helvetica Reising-Uppard"? And why?'

'Let's get her back in bed and I'll talk to you. All about "The Event" –And to answer your question, *we* are Helvetica - and *she* is us. You might think I'm talking a load of gobble-de-gook. But it's one hell of a story, a Donald-Trump-ism, LIKE YOU WOULDN'T BELIEVE, Listen - and listen good, mate. Elvish is responsible for *nothing*. Turn on your recorder, if you like.

1970 – 2021. Before 'The Event'

'It all began in 1970', she said, in her Liverpool twang, 'I was a twenty-year-old – fiercely independent; self-reliant. Never in with the in-crowd, though I partied with, studied with, lots of lads and girls (she said it "gerls"). 'It was coming up to the summer break before my second year at Liverpool

University. A flat for three students was advertised on a handwritten card. Just off Penny Lane, a popular students' hangout. When we moved in, the three of us formed a close friendship. Kindred spirits. Peas in a pod. I became part of our trio-acclaimed 'Three Musketeers' – all for one and one for all.' I was always the "One" in the threesome. Verity and Tricia were the other two-thirds; the ones who named me "Leader of the Pack" "the Alpha"- in our twenties – our seventies– even now in our nineties.

'True, girls?' asked Helen, looking for confirmation. A nod from Verity, a wink from Tricia, in shape-shifting faces.

'From the get-go we hit it off. Liked the same music, the same kind of lads. Loved to dance. Laughed at the same jokes. Loved the sciences, sports, animals.'

'Yeah.' A change of timbre and accent. Cumbrian? 'Worr-aboot me horses? Rode 'em like the wind. Taught these lasses how, an'all.'

'Hi, Verity.' Dr Frank waved. He seemed to be catching on to the differing accents.

'I was a keen horse-rider in Cleator Moor, West Cumbria. Loved the 'Dobbins' and 'Bobbins' that lived in the local stables. where my parents had a small farm. It's mine now, since they passed away. On the boundary of the West Lakes. When we three were there, together, I taught them. We'd ride, get saddle-sore. Three Deadly Horsewomen of the Apocalypse! Me, I'd take a running-jump, swoop up-and-down like a wagtail. Land like a feather on the back of a horse.'

Helen smiled, spoke in Scouse, 'Yep, you're right Verity. And we three were always alike. All blue-eyed. All fair-haired. All no taller than five-foot-four. Freckles on noses.

'We had our differences, of course. Notwithstanding the fact that we three were – still are - joined at the hip.

Tricia nodded. Verity said, 'Aye.' Dr Frank interrupted.

'This is a tad strange, Elvish. I'm watching your eyes change to a variety of blues. Your face-shape alters. Your hair goes curly to wavy to straight. That dimple keeps on appearing and disapp ...'

'Goes with the territory, bonny lad.' Geordie accent.

'Ah, I'm beginning to understand,' Dr Frank said, looking at his notes and photos on the four women. 'Greenish-blue eyes, dimple, north-east accent – Tricia?'

'Yep.'

'Yer startin' to gerr-it, lad.' Helvetica smiled a Helen-smile – wide, sunny, warm.

'Thanks, Helen. The Liverpool accent gave it away.'

'Time for us three old girls t' git some shuteye. See ya later, Doc, wid t' story of t' century.'

'OK, Verity.' Dr Frank laughed.

***

'You alright, Helvetica?' Dr Frank appeared at her bedside.

'Fine. Course I am. Did you get what you wanted from the girls?'

'Well, some of it, I suppose. Nothing about The Event. Doubtless, that'll come later.'

'I'm sure it will. Glad you spoke to them, though. Finally met for real.'

'Mind if I record this? I'm letting you into a little secret here. Give you some insight. Let me be frank. My name is not actually Frank – first or last name. It's Matthew Grey.'

'Oh?' She made a perfect 'O' with her wide mouth, a glimpse of white teeth, generous lips – like Helen's.

'You know, if you twist it, Matthew Grey sounds something like "Grey Matter". Like Hercule Poirot's "little grey cells". Not the sort of name for taking a psychologist seriously. So, because my catch phrase is, "can I be frank", I call myself Dr Frank. It's easier. Makes sense, eh?'

'So why tell me?'

'Changing a name can change a persona. It can change others' perceptions of that person. I'm telling you, because I worked out that Helvetica Reising-Uppard is an anagram. All three of your pals' names shortened and jumbled, Elvish a shortened form. Can't fool me. I do the Guardian crossword.' He winked.

'And that tells you what? I've got this dissociative disorder. Gimme a break.'

'Well - it's a theory. Not necessarily *my* theory:

"But, oh what a tangled web we weave, when first we practise to deceive." So, level with me, Elvish.'

'What about the truth, the whole truth – and nothing but the truth.'

'Touché' Dr Frank held up both hands in surrender, changed the subject.

'How about this narrow boat you live on?'

'Yeah, we live on it most of the year. Up and down the canals, Scotland, England. It's great. They write their books and papers. I do the tech, the publishing. Ever since 2021.'

'So, it's four of you, then? All the time?'

'Yeah, well, since just after "The Event". That's as long as I've known them. You know, it's not really *four*. There's only ever been three. I'm just the bubble wrap. Extra padding. Don't you get that?'

'No, I don't, Elvish.' The doctor's eyes flickered in shadows of sheer disbelief. 'What are you telling me?'

'C'mon, Doc. You need to understand, I'm the outsider. A means to an end.'

'I'm loath to think this is multiple personality disorder in all its glory, Elvish. Maybe, though, if we get to the bottom of this "Event", it will shed some better light.'

'OK. But that's their story to tell. All I can tell you is what they've told me. None of them ever married. Never had kids. They all were the 'only' child. No siblings. All lost their parents by the middle nineties. They only had themselves – and one other. Far as they were concerned, *they* were the only family they had. And for 24 years, I've been an associate – an add-on. 'The Event" changed everything for *them* and introduced *me*.'

'I'll hand you over to Helen and the others. But before I do, Mr Clever Clogs of the Guardian crossword, have you worked out why they call it, "Very-Hellish-Event"?'

'Verity–Helen-Tricia Event. Easy-Peasy.' Doctor Frank smiled. 'Now sleep.'

October 2021 – Leading up to The Event

Helen swallowed loudly before she spoke. She sounded nervous.

'This was going to be a "biggie" for all of us. Best Mates for fifty-one years. Three 71st birthdays in mid-October within a few days of each other.

'Why didn't we celebrate in 2020? COVID, that's why! Remember that nasty pandemic bug, Dr Frank? You might not. Too far in the past, perhaps, from where we are now – twenty-four years on.

'We'd decided to have a "staycation" week in the Lake District. Handy. Not far to travel. Bowness-on-Windermere. A welcome break, after all of us had been stalked and stalled by Covid. Verity came by train from Cumbria. Tricia travelled from Hexham by bus. Me, Helen, 'doing it for myself', I came by car from Liverpool.

'We met up on the third Saturday, at a rented cottage, overlooking Windermere Lake. I'd already aired the house and lit the wood burner. I was warming my hands, when the others arrived.

'I grabbed Verity and Tricia in a huge hug. 'Happy 70th Birthday–Happy 50th Anniversary.' Or 71st and 51st – bloody Covid!

'Out came the wine, the beer, the spirits. All set for an evening clinking glasses, munching snacks, dancing to pop songs – and Hip Hop, our latest fad. Old ladies but still "down with the kids". We laughed and chatted. Shared our memories - over and over.'

'Yeah,' a Cumbrian voice piped up, as Elvish's face altered in her slumber, showing the vivid blue eyes, high cheekbones, rosebud lips and curly fair hair of Verity.

'Ah, Verity. Hello.' Dr Frank waved a welcome toward the dozing body of Elvish on the bed.

'You don't need our life stories, doc. Just the salient stuff. The stuff that has a bearing on that Very-Hellish-Event". From when we three became friends, we spent holidays and weekends together. Still do. I'll tell you a bit about Helen. The stuff that had an impact on the Event.'

'Go on,' said Dr Frank, '...but hang on. You ladies keep interrupting each other. How do you do that? I've never known *that* happen in a Dissociative state before. I didn't think it possible. Three voices, three accents – all at once.'

'Well, doc, maybe because it isn't possible. Maybe it's like we keep trying to tell you.'

'Hmm.'

'So, Dr Frank, let me talk about Helen. Helen is sports mad; played hockey for the Wallasey Women. Good at athletics too, especially the throwing disciplines. She handled the javelin – still does - like an Amazonian warrior; can dance with the discus in imitation of an ancient Greek God – or Wonder Woman.

'Tricia's a different kettle of fish. From Hexham, she's always fancied herself as 'a cut above'.

'Nah,' said Tricia, all high-and-mighty, 'I don't'.

Helen ignored her.

'Her folks are from Money, with a capital 'M'. Cups and certificates in kickboxing. And she could trick a football into fantastic feats. Knee to head to left foot, right foot. Spin toward goal. Bend it like Beckham! Sang like an angel in the church choir - hitting high notes fit to shatter glass.'

'Yeah, lovely. OK, let's get down to the nitty-gritty, guys,' it was Dr Frank's turn to butt in. 'Let's hear about this 'Very-Hellish-Event'.

2021 – Just before The Event

'Right, here goes,' said Tricia, 'You ever heard this rhyme, this song?

"Oh, dear. What can the Matter be – Three Old Ladies locked in a Lavatory"

'Well, that's what happened to us on that 'Event' trip. Our gang of three had spent the first four days taking in the sights, walking in the woods, taking a cruise-boat around Lake Windermere. We basked in the serenity of swans-a-swimming. Laughed at the way they waddled on land, vying for attention and bird food. So relaxing.

On the Thursday, we shopped, expecting we'd have a party in the cottage that night. Saturday morning, we'd be heading back home, needing Friday night to pack up, ready to go.'

Helen intervened. 'Now, our shopping trip is important to the finale of our story, Dr Frank, so listen up. We'd headed to the Mountain Warehouse where Tricia bought us all a spiked hiking stick, didn't you, Trish? Then B & M for snacks and screw-top bottles of wine. I bought a frisbee and a football, for the neighbours' little lad.'

"Yeah, right!" Tricia said, 'For yourself, more like.'

'Then off to a quiet bar on the corner, where we glugged a bottle of wine. "Cheers. To us". Full of aches, pains, grumbles about old age, we headed away toward our lakeside cottage. Let me tell you, I'd been sick of hearing about the "growing old business". More and more, over the years, there were ongoing moans and groans about aging – from them, not me.'

Dr Frank thought, this obviously annoyed Helen, who seemed to be unphased by growing old Said she was sick of hearing:

'Look - wrinkles. All over my face.'

'You can see my Bingo Wings.'

'My boobs are sagging – look!'

It became a bigger dilemma as time marched on, Helen becoming unnerved by the whole thing.

'I'd thought about it again and again,' she said. '*Why does age matter so much.*'

Helen paused. 'You know, guys, for a few days before we went to the Lakes, I'd felt like I was being watched. I kept turning around to see who was behind me. It was weird. Once we were all together in the cottage, I thought the feeling would go away. Only it didn't. It got worse. I wonder ...'

'Wonder what?' asked the psychologist. When he got no answer, he said, 'C'mon, Helen. On with the show.'

'Yeah, where was I?'

'I needed a pee, so Tricia said we should go back to the bar,' Verity chimed in.

'Ah, yes, and I said, No - look, there's a metal lavatory hut. See it? Looks like a silver Tardis.'

'Spooky-looking thing' Verity again.

'Yeah, and I said, "About as spooky as candy floss." I remember crossing the road past pigeons, purring, picking up scraps. And then – ta-dah – we were outside Dr Who's metal receptacle.'

2021 – The Very-Hellish Event

They told it so well. It was as if Dr Frank had been there himself, like a fly on the wall; as though this was The Event, happening in front of his eyes.

***

'Getting dark now. Hurry up." Helen says. "There's a green-lit sign. Look. PRESS TO ENTER. C'mon."

We press. We enter. Heave our rucksacks, tote carrier bags.

It was even more of a Tardis inside than out. Loos to the right, a vestibule to the left, big enough for a posh dinner party. And a huge area straight ahead with a vast console of brightly coloured squares, pushbuttons and computer screens.

"What *is* this?" Tricia sounds like a scaredy-cat.

"Dunno," Verity, eyes radiating terror, "Let's pee and get out – quick."

Helen started to say, "Cool it," but got as far as 'coo…', when a loud, high-pitched, gravelly, other-worldly voice comes over a very buzzy loudspeaker:

DOORS LOCKING. ASSIMILATE TO REJUVENATE

There was a loud CLICK. We ran for the door.

"Oh, god, it's locked." We scream and yell "Lemme Out" to no avail.

"Sod this. I'm off to the toilet. You two get the food and the booze out."

CUTLERY ON THE TABLE. LIFT-OFF. PRESS BLUE TO CONTINUE

"Helen, what should we do?"

DO NOT REFUSE – OR YOU CEASE TO LIVE

Helen shouts from the loo. "Do it, guys - now."

Tricia runs pell-mell to the Console Room. Presses a blue square.

USE THE MALLET

'What? Jeez, it's bloody Wack-a-Mole. OK then, mallet it is.'

A cacophony of high-pitched screams, shrieks and splutters erupts from the loudspeaker.

'Who's that?' Verity wants to know. 'Sounds like Donald Duck and Friends.'

We feel movement – a judder beneath us.

"Are we taking off?" Helen pipes up from the loo, huffing and puffing, pulling up her pants.

"Dunno," Verity shouts an answer, "There's no windows."

"Bugger it! Let's eat, drink and …"

Smoky vapours crawl out from vents in the floor. Heady, potent, like we're being drugged.

"What d'you think you're …" Helen was furious.

GET SEATED TO EAT – DRINK TO THE BRINK – SWEAR, WE DON'T CARE

So we did. To hell with them – whoever they were. Ignoring our captors, we unscrewed bottles of plonk, peeled oranges and kiwis, pronged dates – got comfy.

"Happy Birthday all," Helen toasted, "Cheer up. Sod them. If we're dead, we're dead."

ASSIMILATION IN PROGRESS. NEXT – SUMMON ALEXA.

And we do that too.

'Alexa, play …'

Before long, we're merry as hell, high as kites. Dancing. Singing. Reminiscing.

We boogie to the "Clapping Song", a golden oldie from our past –

Three, six, nine

The goose drank wine

The monkey chewed tobacco on the streetcar line

The line broke, the monkey got choked

And they all went to heaven in a little rowboat

Talking about everything under the sun, we track back to the past – again and again. Inevitably. A favourite threesome handle we'd coined for ourselves after achieving our PhD's – Helen, Psychology; Verity, Psychiatry; Tricia, Philosophy – had been 'the Three Mind Whisperers' - Everything in threes. Just as it ought to be.

We recall funny incidents – laughing, giggling, falling about with merriment.

'What about when we … Remember that time …'

It could be something we remember from yesterday. Or maybe we find ourselves reminiscing about incidents from last month, last year or even the last decade. We devour memories and lap up the past. Sad times, glad times, bad times. The crazy, away-days and holidays.

We talk about how, during the 1980's, we'd separated. Flatmates no more. It was foreseeable; predictable. Home is where the heart is, after all. But, oh how we miss one another when we're apart.

Helen had stayed put in Liverpool, Tricia went northeast to Hexham. Verity galloped off in the direction of West Cumbria.

We must have spent a fortune, before the advent of WhatsApp and Messenger, talking endlessly on the phone about this or that. Our mind-blowing professions. Days gone by. Similarities among us; there were so many things to discuss; to laugh about; to cry about.

Singing, drowsy now, we chant, slow, lazy and drawn-out: ...and we ...all went to ...heaven ...in a little ...rowboat

'Wouldn't that be a lovely thing to do?' Verity sighs. 'Heaven in a rowboat.'

'Think we've been abducted, 'Helen yawns through the unexpected outburst; though there's not a word or a comment from any of us. We drop as one to the floor – falling fast asleep, hardly heeding the sounds of glee from our captors: the madness of badass gremlins, demons, or whatever ...

***

DESTINATION REJUVENATION. ALL FOR ONE. THREE'S A CROWD

'What the hell does that mean?'

We awake, surrounded by orange peel and bits of chocolate cake, empty bottles rolling. We gape – and gasp. Not sure where we are.

'Think we've stopped.'

'What day is it? What time?'

EIGHT O'CLOCK - SATURDAY MORNING

It's the Donald Duck voice from the intercom

ASSIMILATION,
REJUVENATION, COMPLETE.

'I feel sick.' Says Verity to Tricia.

'Blimey – me too – but on a positive, no sign of creaky knees. Like I'm years younger in a funny sort of way.'

'yeah, me an' all. What about you, Helen?'

There's a regurgitation of burps, belches and rancid retching, like a stomping rampage of stomachs and bowels. Hippies coming down from a mix-up of magic mushrooms. All three look aghast. 'Just don't fart,' says Helen.

DOORS UNLOCKING

***

We wriggle around to try and unwrap from a chaos of arm, legs and elbows. Grab our bags. Run for the door. Falling over. Banging heads. Heads? Or Minds?

Yes ... minds – *three* minds. Though it's like our thoughts are overlapping. We recall the chant – "Three's a Crowd", confused as to what the hell these demons/devils/monsters have done to us. Or was it just a prank on their side – and too much booze on ours?

We tumble out of the Tardis, at fever-pitch. Flat on our faces, (one face only?) hurtling our trio of friends around – OW! – in a tangle of limp limbs.

Retaliation. Bash the Bastards. We think as three minds – one brain. One brain? Could it be?

ON DISEMBARKATION, LEAVE YOUR NAME AND COMMENTS.

'Yeah, you bastards.' Helen screams, 'I'll leave comments alright.'

She shouts 'Here's Helen. Having at it with the javelin', glares at seven diminutive beings who look like comical garden gnomes, or Snow White's dwarves, perhaps – and fires a spiked walking stick. It hits a gnome, like a spear. He vanishes – POOF - into the thick fog of a dull morning. She fires again, slamming into another – OOF! Wiped out in the wink of an eye.

Helen calls out to Tricia. 'Your turn, you're up, Trish.'

Quick off the mark, she yells "Gimme the football", grabs the ball in two hands, kicks out with a knee onto the left foot – and strikes. Another gnome bites the dust – WOOSH. The word "Goal" sounds from three voices; the clapping comes from one pair of hands. Strange!

Then Tricia takes a run, performs a roundhouse, kicking a red-hatted gnome in the butt. He disappears in a puff of smoke, trying to hide a split in his yellow trousers - EEEW.

Tricia bellows for Verity.

'Can't do anything. Not me.'

"Yes, you can. Run and jump. Land on them hard - like they're wild horses.'

So, she does. Two in one go, crushes them into the ground - CRRACK…and they fade away.

Verity begins to sing, rolling an empty wine bottle toward the remaining baggy-trousered gnome. Her version of the song …

Hi Ho Hi Ho, It's off to work we go – (the 'hi Ho, hi Ho' line only, in an operatic, soprano voice)

…until the bottle breaks, shattering into a million pieces. Until the final gnome explodes – CLINK-TINKLE.

'Get out of here – NOW!' yells Verity. (Or Helen? Or Tricia? Who knows? Everything's in a muddle – a chaotic mass of disorder)

We run, two arms flapping and flailing, one pair of laboured legs lacking coordination, reaching the pub's picture window.

We stop dead.

Only one person is reflected in the window. A young woman. A blonde-haired, blue-eyed, petite lass. We don't recognise her.

Then Helen does. 'It's US!'

She stares inwardly at "us, ourselves"; pictures us lounging in the amygdala of one brain – one mind. We're all privy to her thinking. All aware each of the three's minds.

'Well,' she says, 'This is a shit storm. You know why it happened?'

Three shakes of one flaxen-haired head in the shop window.

'They wanted to make us young again. Didn't we complain about ageing?

And they made us into one person. Didn't we believe we were like three people in one?

So here we are, "assimilated and rejuvenated". Maybe they meant well – Or maybe we're just an Alien experiment.

Anyway, let's be positive.' "First, we need one name for all three - to incorporate the new fourth member. Have a think'.

We've a sense of what's in one another's minds - 3 + 1= 4, maybe.

There's a crackle, a woosh and an explosion of cartoon-character whoops and hoots. We turn around (as one), look up into a grey, misty-morning sky, watching a shining, silver Tardis, circle above us. Seven red-nosed gnomes sit atop their spaceship, hollering and waving.

BE HAPPY. GO FORTH IN YOUR LITTLE ROW-BOAT. THREE-IN-ONE FOREVER

***

Back to the Future

'We won't bore you with the content of our reply, Dr Frank. However, once we picked a name and a nickname for our newcomer, (you know what they are, Doc) we talked about that "little row-boat" of our Event song. Though a narrowboat would fare us better. Living as one would be a lark.

'Helvetica is crucial to our success in Dropping Off the Face of the Earth in style. She should be congratulated – never dissociated. She's our friend and associate'

At that point, Helvetica (AKA Elvish) woke up with a start.

'Did you get what you needed?' she asked Dr Frank.

'Yes, I did.' Answered the psychologist. 'And on that note, I'm about to discharge you. Go get your hedgehog from the sanctuary – and live your lives.'

Helvetica gave a "whoop", threw her arms in the air and laughed fit to drop.

'We have ourselves a convert, girls. He believes us. Finally. Let's get this show on the road. Hedgehogs to visit. Back to the narrowboat. Articles to write. Books to publish.'

***

KESWICK COURIER - November 2045

Alien Invasion in the Past?

A massive oily stain, found, blasted onto the roadside near Windermere, where a Pay Toilet stood for a short time in that year, 2021. Tests proved that the blast-site appeared to be of a large, square-shaped, alien substance, which had been burned into the ground at highly dangerous temperatures.

Researchers recently, found that the huge blaze-dent, though slightly faded, can still be seen today. The elements discovered at the blast are unknown anywhere, any place, on Earth.

Alien Invaders? Perhaps!

In Bowness-on-Windermere, 2021, a Keswick Courier journalist, now retired, reported a strange sight during a grey, misty, early morning. He gave details of a large rectangular prism, (in the shape of Dr Who's telephone box) leaving the ground, blasting off into Space. He told reporters he saw at least half a dozen garden gnomes waving at the people below. The retired journalist now resides in a local care home for the elderly. When asked for a quote, he refused to comment.

Afterword & Acknowledgements

I t seems strange and rather wonderful to get to this stage of my 'Strange Tales are These' short story collection. The end – phew! - aaah!

All the stories written, typed – and edited, edited, edited. All the boxes ticked (I think – I hope). Ready to "rock n roll" as they say. What a peculiar feeling.

I've spent my time and paid my dues to writing groups and blogs, over decades, here, there and everywhere. I've submitted entries to competitions over the years, managing to collect a few wins online. I'm far from dissatisfied, especially after biting the bullet and getting published a couple of times in Small Press anthologies. Writing a double-page feature for a national magazine, was a massive highlight, albeit many moons ago.

There've been times when I felt the need to give writing a break (too many times, it must be said) because of work commitments or family commitments or health problems.

Well, here I am, at last – a "published author". I couldn't have done it without a nudge and a shove from lots of people along the way. It all took much more than a hop and a skip. So, to every one of you who've helped, pushed and prodded, I can only say,

'Thank you, thank you, thank you – all of you. I finally did it, after such a long journey.'

I wish I could give a mention to all the folks who've motivated and supported me over the years, notwithstanding the lengthy ups and downs of my writing history. There are those who've just been there for me, through thick and thin. You know who you are. TA very much, guys.

~

To Leah Stuart, my talented, gorgeous niece (tho' not an actual relative!) thank you for the splendid illustration sitting proudly on the front cover of 'Strange Tales'. It's a true work of art, you clever person, you. The picture tells the tale of the first story in this anthology, entitled, 'it's Raining Cats and Dogs'. The animals are such true likenesses of her pet dogs and my cats, it almost takes my breath away. Kudos to you, Leah. One day soon, I'll make it right and contribute to the learning disabilities charity you work for. I will!

To North Tyneside Council's Creative Writing Group (Monday afternoons, in North Shields Library in School Term time) run and tutored by the amazing Amanda Robson, Thank You! Cheers for the themes, the resources, the critiquing sessions, the support, the free writing opportunities – and the ever-existence of camaraderie. I might have jacked it all in, had it not been for you all.

There are moves afoot, via one of our group, to collect, compile and publish a poetry and short story collection of our contributions later in the year. So watch this space.

In October/November 2024, joining a six week "Fiction Foundations" course with New Writing North (NWN), I truly found my writing feet (or, more to the point, *fingers*). What a super-duper outfit New Writing North are. The fact that they have their base in Newcastle is an amazing thing for the city and its environs. For that, (personally and for the whole northeast of England), a great big thank you. We in Geordieland are the luckiest authors and wannabee writers in the world.

The NWN Fiction Foundations course tutor, Mike Hollows, is the epitome of fantastic teaching and mentorship. He's a great author too, writing as Mike J Hollows. Look him up! He was a marvellous tutor/mentor of our cohort. His critiques and feedback are always second to none. Thank you, Mike – so much.

Participating on the same course, we discovered that several of us live in the North Tyneside area. We met up, formed a writing group – and the rest, they say, is history! We meet at least once a month to catch up and talk all things writing. We do regular 'Sit and Write' sessions in various local cafes. And, apart from our own writing projects, we've launched a writing blog, entitled: Northern Wordsmiths. There, although still in its infancy, you can read some of our (what I call) Blog Bits! Please do pop in, take a look - and comment. Don't miss it. There's some really great writing and off-beat stories.

Find us on: northernwordsmiths.com

... or Facebook GROUP - Northern Wordsmiths
... or read about our blog project online, via NWN @ *www.profwritingacademy.com/waging-a-war-on-writers-block*

What I would do without this fantastic group, I don't know. You made me see the light at the end of the writing tunnel, guys. Ellen, Liam and Chelsea, you rock!

Then of course, there's designer and publisher Jay Thompson of UK Book Publishing in Whitley Bay who has put up with me and my foibles throughout this whole process, guiding me over the bumps, despite all my blind spots and occasional deaf ears. He looks so young (like he's about twelve!) but has the demeanour and gravitas of a very wise man. And a great sense of humour. I hang on your every word, Jay.

Last, but sure as hell not least, Dave Hildreth, husband, friend and love of my life. What can I say? Well, I'm not going to say anything very much, because you'll get all high and mighty and arrogant. And there's enough of that in this family, what with all the self-centredness and haughtiness of our two gorgeous-but-supercilious cats, Daisy May and Jeremiah (Jerry). Take it from me, Dave, you're a little bit better-behaved than either cat. And, let's face it, you're much more well-behaved than I am at the best of times – or even the worst of times!

So …Thanks for everything. Thanks for being you. Please don't let this accolade go to your head.

Naturally, good readers, I couldn't possibly draw a line under this section without saying 'Thanks a Million' for buying/reading/borrowing the book. I hope you've enjoyed my story collection.

You might consider following me wherever and whenever you like. Only if it takes your fancy. Maybe we'll meet again sometime.

About the Author

Sheila was "seeded" in Liverpool, "budded" in West Cumbria and "blossomed" in Newcastle upon Tyne.

After careers in secretarial, nursing and teaching FE students, she's come out the other end as an 'emerging writer'. How she can possibly be just 'emerging' at such a ripe old age is anyone's guess! Yet, here she is, eventually, having travelled down the road of becoming a published author.

If what you're looking to read is 'sugar and spice and all things nice', this collection of six short stories is certainly not for you, but if you're looking for 'spiders and snakes and puppy dogs' tails (tales), then this is, for sure, your cup of tea.

Sheila used to write, under the name, Sheila Newton, at the beginning of the 'Teenies', with some mild victories online, also a 'glossy' magazine article – and in a Small Press magazine. After a break in writing of at least a decade, here she is again. But with the triumph of social media over the years, there are a small number of Sheila Newton's out there, as authors online. So, as befits an emerging author, her pen name has changed to –

Sheila LaNewton

Hope you enjoy 'Strange Tales are These'.